to:

C0-AWE-522

Mr. Euan Ker Cameron,

a gift from the

author

March 29, 2005

The Serpent's Empire

Satan, Yesterday and Today

Joaquin Caminero Guerrero, M.D.

VANTAGE PRESS
New York

The dust jacket shows: above and right, two famous Egyptian pyramids; above and center, the Santo Domingo's Pyramid (the pyramid-tomb of Christopher Columbus); above and left, the famous pyramid "El Castillo" in Central America; below and left, the Kremlin in Moscow with the Lenin's pyramid (the tomb of V.I. Lenin); below and center, an ancient Egyptian pharaoh sacrificing a person to a pagan god; below and right, the symbol of U.S.A., an eagle with a band in the beak, the band represents a serpent, this American eagle is a way of representing the Egyptian "winged solar-disc" (the symbol of the Serpent-God, Satan and the Son-God), at the top of the dust jacket.

Cover design by Awards A Plus LLC New York © March 2001
(The text of this book does not reflect the opinions of the people of Awards A Plus)

FIRST EDITION

All rights reserved, including the right of
reproduction in whole or in part in any form.

Copyright © 2002 by Joaquin Caminero Guerrero, M.D.

Published by Vantage Press, Inc.
516 West 34th Street, New York, New York 10001

Manufactured in the United States of America
ISBN: 0-533-13876-0

Library of Congress Catalog Card No.: 01-126119

0 9 8 7 6 5 4 3 2 1

BLESSED IS THE ONE WHO READS.
        —John, Apocalypse 1:3

YOU WILL KNOW THE TRUTH, AND THE TRUTH WILL MAKE YOU FREE.
        —Jesus Christ, John 8:32

YOU SHALL LOVE GOD . . . AND YOUR NEIGHBOR.
        —Jesus Christ, Matthew 22:37 and 38

YOU SHALL NOT KILL.
        —Jesus Christ, Mark 10:19

Contents

Introduction, Part One

Millions of human beings have died in wars, rebellions, and genocides in the last five thousand years in all the world. Most of them have died in order to satisfy the ambition of men in power. These are: Pharaohs, kings, emperors, princes, presidents, dictators, popes, and others. Most of those people died because the religion of many of these rulers was satanism, which has been practiced in public (like the Aztec rulers) or semi-hidden. Most of those dead ignored the fact that their governors were Satanists. Perversions and injustices have been the rule in almost all the planet. The perversions are huge and in crescendo in modern times. Wars, genocides, and perversions could be avoided if we had followed the teachings of Jesus Christ. But the teachings of the Bible (and Christ) have been ignored, occulted, and distorted by men in power, the governors, and the Vatican, and for this reason, the planet has been a bitter place for living for most of mankind.

The blood of the dead claim that it is time to say the truth: they all died because many of the rulers and religious leaders were and are Satanists. This book is my effort to expose the ancient and modern satanism. It is a very infrequent thing to listen to something about Satan; many speak about him as if he doesn't exist. The readers of this book will be surprised to know that the Serpent (Satan) is everywhere, every day, and almost no one takes notice of him.

This is a book of analysis, I analyzed the religious and political life of ancient civilizations, and also I analyzed the Bible and the Koran. The religious practice of ancient people is analyzed in this book according to narrations and teachings of the Bible. Whoever wants to analyze the Bible has to mention the books and verses that he is studying. This is the right way of doing theology. Therefore I mentioned many verses of the Bible and the Koran without quoting them because I studied them in the Spanish version (my native language), and it is not a proper thing to quote words and sentences that are in another language, especially in the case of the Bible. But in none of the verses mentioned did I change the meaning. It should be known that there are few differences in some verses in different versions and translations of the Bible; one of the reasons is that there are several "original" Bibles with some differences. For example, some Bibles never mention the word "obelisk" and others do so (the Book of Jeremiah).

The Bible that I have been reading and studying for approximately twenty-five years is the *Catholic Bible,* translated by Eloino Nacar and Alberto Colunga, seventh edition of 1957. In order to do this research, I also used about ten Bibles (Catholic and non-Catholic). The quotation marks that I used (" ") when mentioning a verse indicate the beginning and the ending of the verse (so the readers can notice and differentiate the opinion of the Bible or the Koran from my opinion), but I am not quoting letter by letter any verse from any Bible or Koran. Some words or an entire verse are in capital letters. They are not in this manner in the books I studied; I wrote them in capital letters to highlight their importance.

The book is divided in two parts: the first part refers to the satanism of ancient times and the second is on the same topic in modern times. The information and the secrets exposed and revealed in this book are the result of a bibliographic research and a careful and detailed study of the Bible and the Koran. The investigation was carried only by me and took me nine years to do it (from 1989 to 1998).

I am a Christian. I am opposed to all kind of hate, violence, or abuse (physical, verbal, or psychological). No one should use my ideas to exercise violence against any other person or his property. As a Christian, medical doctor, and pathologist, I carried out this investigation using the basic fundamentals of the scientific method and the teachings of Jesus Christ: the search, acquisition, and exposition OF THE TRUTH.

JOAQUIN CAMINERO GUERRERO
(YSSDCLEDOFYTF
EEEAQDVYEVQSHC)
June 8, 1999
West Palm Beach
Florida, USA

Introduction, Part Two

The Wise King Solomon Is the Apocalyptic Beast 666 (Apocalypse 13:18 is based on 1 Kings 10:14)

Summary of the book *The Serpent's Empire: Satan, Yesterday and Today*, written by Dr. Joaquin Caminero Guerrero, medical doctor, pathologist, certified by Columbia University of New York, USA. The author is Christian and Catholic.

All the continents of the ancient world were governed by rulers who believed in Satan's laws: human sacrifices, obelisks, and pyramid building, worship of the "Serpent-god," astrology and worship of the "Sun-god." This satanic "religion" arose in Sumer and Egypt and from here was spread to the whole world including America (this Satanism arrived into America approximately four thousand years ago, therefore Columbus didn't discover America). Around the year 1000 before Christ and in the first century of the Christian era, arose and was consolidated a satanic group headed by the Jews' King David, his son Solomon, and by Paul ("Saint Paul"). These three persons believed in the satanic faith confession written in Genesis 3:1–6, here Satan said to Eve about the forbidden tree "No, you won't die, God knows that the day you eat of it your eyes will be open and you will be like God, knowing good and evil," and Eve realized that the tree was good "to reach wisdom. . . ." This satanic confession of faith was repeated by David, Solomon, and Paul as written in the following verses in the Bible:

1. 2 Samuel 14:17 and 20, about David, a person said: "my king is like an angel of God to distinguish good from evil. . . . But my king is wise, with the wisdom of an angel of God."
2. 1 Kings 3:9, Solomon asks "God": "give to your servant a prudent heart to judge your people and distinguish between good and evil"; verse 3:12 says that "God" said to Solomon, "I give you a wise and intelligent heart."
3. Hebrews 5:10–13 (a letter from Paul to the Hebrews) contains Paul's satanic confession of faith (the satanic oath): "About that we have much to say, of difficult understanding . . . " to teach again "to distinguish between good and evil." Paul's Satanism is also exposed in 2 Peter 3:15 and 16: ". . . our beloved brother Paul wrote you according to the wisdom that was given to him. . . ."

These satanic confessions of faith are written in the Bible only in these verses: Genesis 3:1–6 (Satan), 2 Samuel 14:17 and 20 (David), 1 Kings 3:9 (Solomon), Hebrews 5:10–13 (Paul) and Ecclesiasticus 17:6.

The Satanist Luke ("Saint Luke") even knowing that Christ rejected the "Wisdom" and only approved "the Law and the Prophets," said about Christ: "The Boy was growing up full of wisdom"; read Luke 2:40. (Remember that the Old Testament is divided into three parts: the Law, the Prophets, and the books of Wisdom). James, Christ's brother, wrote: there is an "animal, demonic wisdom," read James 3:15.

The Apocalypse (Revelation) is not a book about the future, but a book about history in which John exposed (revealed) the quasi-hidden Satanism of David, Solomon, and Paul ("Saint Paul"). For example: Apocalypse 13:18 says: "Here is the wisdom. The one who is intelligent reckons the number of the beast, because it is the number of a man. His number is 666."

This verse contains the clues (keys) to decipher the puzzle; the answer is in 1 Kings 10:14: "The weight of the gold that every year came to Solomon was 666 talents of gold." The concordance between the two verses is:

Apocalypse 13:18	1 Kings 10:14
"Here is the wisdom"	In "Solomon" (who represents the wisdom)
is a "man"	"Solomon"
"his number is 666"	"666"

The number 666 only appears in the Bible in four verses. John wrote the Apocalypse taking ideas from the Old Testament.

The other beast in the Apocalypse is David (the King) and the false prophet is Nathan (David and Solomon's prophet). David and Solomon are the spiritual fathers of the Jewish Satanists and the Freemasons. The "Antipas" of Apocalypse 2:13 is Herod Antipas, who was the Jews' governor of Jerusalem when Christ ("my faithful witness") was killed. The "letters" to the churches written in Apocalypse are like a charade game: they refer to Paul who also wrote "letters" to the churches. Apocalypse 2.5 says: "Consider from where you have fallen . . .," and Apocalypse 3:18 says: I will give you "salve to put on your eyes, so you can see . . .," both verses refer to Paul, who "fell to the ground" and after that remained blind for a few days. The Vatican was created basically following Paul's teaching. The Vatican also has helped the Jewish Satanists and the Freemasons to keep in secret the real identity of the beast 666, because they are all Satanists.

The Jewish Satanists created groups, revolutions and governments under Satan's law, for example: the Knight's Templars, the Crusaders, the French, North American, and Soviet revolutions, the "independence" of the Latin American republics; by these reasons: Lenin is buried in a pyramid, Karl Marx believed in the satanic confession of faith when Marx exposed his theory about the struggle of the "opposite" (the good and evil), the dollar has a drawing of a pyramid, the Latin American flags include satanic-Masonic symbols (pyramids, serpents, Phrygian caps, suns, etc.), the Washington Monument is an obelisk (Washington was a mason), Simon Maccabee, beloved Jew (beloved by the followers of Judaism) built pyramids according to the biblical book 1 Maccabees 13:28: "Above he built seven pyramids."

Muhammad, creator of the Muslim "religion," also believed in the satanic confession of faith as written in his book the Koran, chapter 2, verse 181: "The month of Ramadan, during which the Koran was sent from above to be a guide for man, to explain clearly the precepts, and to distinguish between good and evil. . . ." Muhammad also said in the Koran that "God" gave wisdom to David and Solomon and that "God" will punish Christ because Christ rejected the wisdom. The Mormons also believed in the satanic confession of faith (Hellaman 14:31, Moses 6:56, and 2 Nephi 2:26, the Book of Mormon).

The secret and mysterious words written in the Koran: Sin, Nun, Sad, Lam, Mim, etc., were copied from the David's Psalms 9, 10, 25, 34, 37, etc., which also proves that Muhammad was another Davidian Satanist, follower of the satanic doctrine of "wisdom." Hitler and the Nazis were also Satanist.

In modern times the Freemasons and other hermetic groups are responsible for the Satanism that controls all the world governments.

In short, the following is the history of Satanism: Sumer—Egypt—Phoenicia—Mayan, Aztecs, Incas—David and Solomon—Paul/Luke—the Vatican—Muhammad—the Knights Templars—the Freemasons—the French, North American, and Soviet revolutions—current governments of the world.

The Serpent's Empire

Part One

1. Satan, Yesterday and Today

A long time ago, Satan (also called the Serpent, Dragon, and Devil), was defeated in a battle by Michael and his angels. After this battle, the Serpent was precipitated to Earth. After Satan arrived on Earth, he spent several centuries building a world-wide empire, which had the following primary characteristics:

1. on several continents the people built pyramids,
2. in those nations the people considered the serpent as a symbol of a "god" and worshiped this "serpent god,"
3. the people of those countries made human sacrifices; at the top of hundreds of pyramids during several centuries, they committed human sacrifices to honor this Serpent; many of the sacrificers used to eat the flesh of the sacrificed,
4. some of the peole of those nations had knowledge of astronomy and practiced astrology,
5. many people of those nations used drugs during religious ceremonies to produce altered mental states, and
6. they considered the sun as a "god," and the rulers considered themselves as "sons" of the "sun-god."

It is the Bible that gave us the different names of Satan. The Christian tradition teaches that God opposed the above six characteristics of the ancient civilizations. The beliefs of this religion that followed the God of Abraham says that the Israelites were forbidden to build altars of polished stone (among them the pyramids). Also it was forbidden to worship the Serpent; it was forbidden to make human sacrifices, to practice astrology, and to use hallucinogenic drugs.

These are some of the ancient people who had some or all of these six characteristics: Hindus, Chinese, Babylonians, Egyptians, Phoenicians, Romans, Mayans, Incas, and the Aztecs. The ancient world was not formed by non-communicating continents. The Satanists of ancient time traveled throughout the world, spreading their criminal beliefs.

It was Satan who taught those nations "knowledge" and a criminal "wisdom," which the people used to build their cities and satanic civilizations characterized by the above six. What God taught to the Israelite peoples were knowledge and wisdom that led the humans to establish among them health, love, and peace.

¤   ¤   ¤

There was a worldwide empire in ancient times, governed by the satanic religion. There were not many religions in ancient times. There were only two religions: the satanic and the true religion of those who followed the God of Abraham. From one nation to another, there was some variation in the satanic religion, but the basic beliefs were the same. The true religion was taught to the humans as soon as they were created, but Satan made them forget the holy law and they learned the perversions that he taught to the humans. The Bible speaks extensively about the holy law and the struggle of the followers of God against satanic belief. The Bible is not only a book that teaches love and peace, it is also a book of history, which describes the abomination and the most important characteristics of the Serpent's World Empire.

The fundaments of the satanic religion and the serpent's empire were born in Mesopotamia (in Sumer; the Babylonians were descendants of the Sumerians) and in Egypt, from there they were taken to Phoenicia and from there to America. To the east it was spread to India and to the Mongolian people. It is not a coincidence that the Bible emphasizes the terrible condemnation against Mesopotamia, Egypt, and Phoenicia.

✿   ✿   ✿

Wherever there were pyramids, there was the worship of the serpent, and this was considered a symbol of a "god." Currently, there are groups that adore the pyramids and the serpent. For that reason we see in the one-dollar bill a drawn pyramid and serpents in a subliminal manner. Pyramids and serpents are not symbols of the Christian religion; therefore to which "god" is addressed in the words written on the dollar bill: "In God We Trust"? In this book I will explain the god to whom these words are addressed. Persons and groups of different backgrounds in our time are characterized by practicing one or more of the six satanic characteristics already mentioned. Among them are the Theosophists, Rosicrucians, astrologists, occultists, gnostics, individual persons, and Freemasons. The Freemasons are a special group due to the immense number of them, but overall because they are a powerful group (economically and politically) with worldwide ramifications. They used their power to make the French Revolution, the North American revolution, the independence of the Latin American countries (including the Dominican Republic), and the Communist revolution in Russia.

One of the most terrible characteristics of the Freemasons is the secrecy they keep about their beliefs and activities, to the point that few people in the Dominican Republic know that Juan Pablo Duarte (the founding father of the Dominican nation) was a Mason, and few know that his project of national independence was part of the worldwide goal of the satanic

Freemasonry. Few Dominicans know that the first national shield included the drawing of a serpent (the representation of Satan) and a Phrygian cap, which was one of the symbols used by the French Revolutionaries. Few people of every country know that with their own eyes they see daily Masonic symbols without realizing it. Another clear and eloquent example is that few Dominicans know that the Columbus Lighthouse is a pyramid built by International Freemasonry in order to honor Satan. The Columbus Lighthouse is a very expensive and enormous monument supposedly built to honor Columbus and his discovery of the New World; the discovery of America is called by the Freemasons and others "the encounter of two cultures;" obviously the Masons know that America was not discovered by Columbus, but by the ancient Egyptian and Phoenician Satanists who were predecessors of the current Freemasons. Today few persons know that during the French Revolution the Christian religion was eliminated and replaced by "the religion of Reason" (a name given by the Satanists to the ancient "wisdom" that was taught by Satan in ancient time according to the Book of Genesis in the Bible). In Mexico, Christians were persecuted during the Reform, which was led by a Mason, Benito Juarez.

✿   ✿   ✿

We know that the ancient world was pagan, idolatrous, sinful, and perverted, and the minds of almost all humans were in darkness, chained by Satan. When I use the word "empire" to describe the reign of the Serpent, I say that the rulers of the ancient nations knew that they were obeying the law of the Devil, and they used their religious, military, and economic power to create and maintain nations, with both government and population being followers of the law of Satan. In this book I will explain the remote and modern history of the Serpent's Empire.

2. Satan at the Beginning of Time

The following verses of the Apocalypse are very important to understand that: Satan is an entity with supernatural power, that he came from the sky to earth full of hate, and that he is called Serpent and Dragon, reasons that explain the six primary characteristics of the Serpent's Empire.

Apocalypse 12, verses 7, 8, and 9 say: "There was a battle in the sky; Michael and his angels fought against the dragon, and the dragon and his angels also fought, and they couldn't triumph, and his place in the sky wasn't found. The big dragon was thrown out, the ancient serpent, also called Devil and Satan, that deceived the whole round earth, and he was thrown down to the earth, together with his angels."

Apocalypse 12:12 says: "By this, rejoice, heaven and those who live there. Woe to the earth and the sea! for the Devil has come down to you full of anger, because he knows that he has little time left." Verse 20:1 says, "I saw an angel coming down from heaven, bringing the key of the abyss and a great chain in his hand. He seized the dragon, the ancient serpent, who is the devil, Satan, and he chained him for one thousand years." There is no doubt about the identity of the Serpent.

Those are some of the Bible verses about the origin of Satan. The traditions of most of the ancient nations speak about a being considered a "god" and represented by a serpent, which can be confirmed by reading the history of ancient people. Those traditions do not say where Satan came from, and they don't say the reasons why Satan came to earth. The Bible does not deny what those traditions say about the serpent or the dragon. The Bible admits the existence in the pagan tradition of beings represented by the serpent or dragon. But the holy book contains more and better information about the devil and adds, for example, that the serpent is also called Dragon, Satan, and Devil, that the "devil" is "homicidal" since the beginning (Saint John 8:44), and that the serpent is an enemy of the human race and God (Genesis 3:14–19). The Bible makes a negative moral judgment about the serpent, while the ancient people adored that serpent. The Asians adore Satan under the concept of the Dragon.

The Bible says ("suggests" is a better word) that Satan was an angel. This fallen angel came to earth and there was dedicated to build an empire, which included several continents, among them America, Africa, and Asia. The date the empire began is difficult to establish with precision, but there are some facts that can help to determine that date. For example, the first pyramid built on the planet was around the year 2670 B.C. Human creation happened possibly around 3760 B.C., it is pending investigation whether the six days of the creation were days or millions of days. Between the human creation and the construction of the first pyramid, Satan came to the earth; that means between 3760 and 2670 B.C. The use of the serpent as a symbol dates back approximately to the year 3000 B.C.; therefore this date is more appropriate to calculate the arrival of Satan. Therefore, Satan came to the earth between 3760 and the year 3000 B.C.. This date of the Creation has been questioned. We will have a more precise date of the creation when the length of the six days of creation is fully clarified.

Knowing the already mentioned apocalyptic verses, we know the reason why the ancient people made human sacrifices, knew astronomy, and represented the devil as a serpent. Satan came to earth full of hate, taught his hate to the humans, and also taught them to make human sacrifices and eat the flesh of the sacrificed. He came from heaven and for this, he has wide knowledge of astronomy and supernatural power, and he is called Serpent.

At the time of building the empire, the worshipers of Satan left signs of him on temples and pyramids: sculpted and drawn serpents.

Other verses of the Apocalypse that are important are 12:3 and 4, which say that "another sign appeared in heaven, and I saw a great dragon with the color of fire, with his tail swept down a third of the stars of heaven and threw them to the earth." There is no doubt that Satan came from heaven to the earth with his angels.

Any person, whether atheist or religious, who reads the history of ancient civilization and learns that those nations built pyramids, made human sacrifices, worshiped the serpent, and knew astronomy, those readers will be aware of the truth and will admit that the Bible says the truth because in the holy book, there is abundant data about the religious beliefs of those civilizations. When reading the Bible and at the same time books about the ancient civilizations, it is very easy to recognize that there was a world empire ruled by Satan.

Almost every ancient civilization has legends about a "god" who taught them different arts. Genesis 4:20–22 describes several skills of the descendants of Cain. For example, tent dwelling, to have livestock, playing the lyre and pipe, and making tools of bronze and iron. Cain gave his soul to the devil when he killed Abel; as a reward Satan taught his descendant those arts. Since the time the dragon came to earth, he wished to teach the human being a wisdom that did not come from God. It is said in Genesis 3:1–6 that the serpent appeared to Eve and told her that she would acquire knowledge about good and evil, and "wisdom," if she obeyed him. The Egyptians say that the god Osiris taught them to be civilized. Osiris (Satan, or one of his demons) traveled throughout the world, "civilizing" people.

Some American tribes believed that the "god" Quetzalcoatl taught them knowledge and wisdom. In Babylon, people believed the same about the "god" Oannes. In America the "sun-god" ordered Manco Capac (the "first" Inca) to bring civilization to the Indian. According to the Sumerians, the "god" Enki taught the humans several arts. Another Egyptian "god" considered a civilizer was Ptah.

The Bible and the satanic book the Koran say clearly that Satan and his demons gave knowledge and wisdom to human beings. The Koran says the following: "The demons teach men magic and the science that descended from above over the two angels of Babel, Harut and Marut" (Sura II, verse 96); different Koran's translations have different verse numbers; this story and the story of the Tower of Babel in the Bible imply that it was to the Babylonians (or to their ancestors, the Sumerians) that Satan first taught. The Koran continues, saying that "the men learned from them the way to create discord between man and woman and that the men learned about what was bad for them and not those things that are useful, and they knew that the one who had bought this art had no part in the future life." The same verse of the Sura says about the demons: "these did not instruct anyone in his art without saying: we are the temptation." Satan is the tempter, the accuser, the murderer since the beginning; these demons did not hide their identity when they taught the human. The Koran continues, saying that "THE WINE AND THE STATUES ARE AN ABOMINATION CREATED BY SATAN," AND THAT "THE FALSE DIVINITY SUGGESTED THE IDEA OF KILLING THEIR OWN CHILDREN." (Sura 5:92 and 6:138). The writer of the Koran says: "In another time the people formed one single nation" (Sura II verse 209). The same says that of the Bible when talking about the Tower of Babel. It should be known that the Koran is a book "sent to corroborate the Jewish scripture" (Sura 2 verse 38) and also: "destined to confirm the holy books;" that means the Jewish Scripture (Sura 2-91).

There is no doubt that Satan taught human beings to make human sacrifices. The Bible speaks in 1 Timothy 4:1 about: the "teaching of the demons," and Ecclesiasticus 19:20 says that: "THERE IS AN EXECRABLE WISDOM," which is the one that came from Satan. The Book of Job says in chapter 12:7 and 8: "Ask the beast, and they will teach you; . . . ask the reptiles of the earth and they will instruct you"; with the knowledge of cause, the authors of these three books say this, because as I will show you in this book, they are Satanists (the point is that they admit that the Serpent "teaches" wisdom). The people of Israel did not receive knowledge or wisdom about pyramids and human sacrifices, but knowledge and wisdom about improving human behavior.

3. Satan, Builder of Pyramids

It is very easy to realize that after Satan came to earth, he created or built an empire, which included distant regions situated in Africa, Asia, and America; the proof is in the fact that almost all the ancient nations adored the serpent and built pyramids in which they sculpted or drew serpents.

In Egypt there are about ninety-five pyramids. The first, called the Zoser Pyramid, was built around 2670 B.C. In Babylon there were pyramids called ziggurats. In India there are pyramids (or temples with a pyramidal shape) among them: the temple of Ellora, and the one in Madurai, in Kanchipuran, and the temple of Buddh-Gaya. In America there are hundreds of pyramids, and some historians believe that some of those pyramids date back to the first or second century B.C., for example, the Mayan pyramid called E-VII-sub; in this pyramid there are structures that look like the heads of serpents. In Java, Indonesia, there are pyramids also. There are pyramids in the Canary Islands; when Europeans arrived in these islands before the time of Columbus, they found that the natives (the *"guanches"*) were white with blue eyes some of them, but the natives did not have ships and did not remember the reason and the century they went to those islands; the truth is that the Phoenicians took them to those islands. There are pyramids in China also.

No one should believe that the existence of pyramids on different continents was the spontaneous and independent products of those ancient people. The Phoenicians, following the wishes of Satan, came to America and brought all the satanic knowledge, including the building of pyramids and the human sacrifices. The Phoenicians were a people of the pre-Christian era; they were famous Satanists who lived on the coast of the Mediterranean Sea in what today is Lebanon. They were famous seafarers and colonizers. The Phoenician city called Sidon was at its height between the year 2300 and 1290 B.C. Phoenicians from the Mediterranean Sea sent an expedition to distant points, including the Canary Islands in the Atlantic Ocean near the African coast (circa 450 B.C.), and around all of the African and European coasts, including the coast of England. Sailing the African coast, they reached Zimbabwe where they looked for gold. These Phoenicians had as one of their main industries, the production and commercialization of a purple dye extracted from a marine shell. They brought to America the searching for this marine shell, to the pre-Columbian Amerindian who kept this practice (the searching of the shells) and for this reason the Amerindians put on the walls of some pyramids the marine shell, which can be seen today on those pyramids. The Phoenicians had a close relationship with the powerful Egyptians from whom they learned the satanic religion, and they spread this religion to the continents they visited. The Bible and the archaeology tell us that the Phoenicians were pagans who loved the sacrifice of children.

The arrival of iron in ancient Egypt and the acquisition of horses and the wheel by Egyptian authorities occurred between the year 1600 and 1300 B.C. This indicates that around this date the Phoenicians and Egyptians stopped traveling to America, and I say this because when Columbus arrived in America, he found that the Amerindians did not have horses, the wheel, or iron. The great Pyramid of Giza in Egypt was built by Cheops (between 2589 and 2566 B.C.), which indicates that the power of the Pharaohs was immense at this time; this power allowed them to go to America, so we can estimate approximately the time the Phoenicians and Egyptians were traveling to America, and this time was between the twenty-seventh or twenty-sixth centuries and the thirteenth century B.C..

The study of DNA (deoxyribonucleic acid), including the mitochondrial DNA in Amerindians, will shed clear evidence about the arrival of Phoenicians, Egyptians, and Africans to America in times before Jesus Christ. The marine archaeology will show the presence of Phoenician and Egyptian artifacts (and possibly Phoenician ships) on the American coast. We should know that the legend of Hiram Habif is one of the pillars of Freemasonry; this Hiram was a pagan from the Phoenician city of Tyre, according to the Bible. We will talk later about this Hiram Habif.

✿   ✿   ✿

As we know, the pyramids and the ancient pagan temples are made of stones that were cut so that one fits securely with the other; some pyramids were made of bricks. These facts were known by the biblical writers and based on this, they used the words "polished stone" to refer to the building of temples by pagans. Wherever there were pyramids, there was the worship of the serpent or the dragon, and they were considered symbols of a "god." There are abundant verses in the Bible that speak negatively about the building of monuments and statues made of polished stone. God recommended to the Israelites not to build temples of polished stone because that was a practice of the ancient people, as part of their satanic beliefs. The opposition of the Bible to the building of those temples includes the pyramids, which were made of polished stone and besides, they are the *sui generis* of the satanic temple (at the top of the pyramids, millions of human sacrifices were committed to honor the serpent).

The first recorded action of God against the pyramid was the action against the Tower of Babel, according to Genesis

11:1–9). The Satanists used this case to argue that God is the bad entity because he did not allow the human beings "to reach heaven," using the stairs or tower-pyramid and the rites and the satanic "mysteries" associated with the pyramids. What those Satanists don't want to say is that the prohibition "to reach heaven" was ordered precisely because their "god" was the Serpent, which requested the making of human sacrifices in those pyramids, which conducted the sacrificers to the inferno and not to heaven. The "builders" did not believe and do not believe in God or Jesus who say "I am the way, the truth and the life" (John 14:6). Jesus Christ is the way to reach heaven; the way and stairs of the "builders" and "architects" are the laws of the Dragon: human sacrifices, hallucinogens, astral projections, pyramids, the Egyptian "mysteries," etc. It is believed that this Tower of Babel was one of the pyramids called a ziggurat, in Babylon. THE CASE OF THE TOWER OF BABEL CLEARLY INDICATES THAT THE CONSTRUCTION OF PYRAMIDS DOES NOT COME FROM GOD NOR FROM GOD'S FOLLOWERS, BUT FROM SATAN.

God did not like the Egyptian religion that had the six characteristics already mentioned, which include the building of pyramids. We read that in Leviticus 18.3 in which God says, "YOU SHALL NOT DO AS THEY DO IN THE LAND OF EGYPT, where you have lived, and you shall not do as they do in the land of Canaan . . . do not follow their custom" (where they followed the law of Satan). Leviticus 26:1 says "Don't make idols, and don't erect carved pillars, and you shall not place in your land carved stone to worship them, because I AM, Yahweh, your God." First Maccabees 4:42, 43, and 47 talk about the reestablishment of the worship of the true God in Israel: "They choose blameless priests, lovers of the Law, which purify the temple and throw away the stones of the idolatric altar, to an unclean place, and took non-carved stone, according to the Law; they repaired the sanctuary and the interior of the temple."

We should know that one of the Maccabees disobeyed the Law and built tomb-pyramids in Israel according to 1 Maccabees 13:27 and 28, which say the following about the pyramids built by Simon Maccabees an Israelite leader: "Simon built a monument over the tomb of his father and brothers made of carved stone on all sides, tall and visible from far away. HE ALSO ERECTED SEVEN PYRAMIDS, ONE IN FRONT OF THE OTHER, DEDICATED TO HIS FATHER, TO HIS MOTHER, AND TO HIS FOUR BROTHERS." Deuteronomy 27:5 and 6 say, "you will build there an altar to Yahweh, AN ALTAR OF STONE IN WHICH YOU HAVE NOT USED AN IRON TOOL; YOU MUST BUILD THE ALTAR TO YAHWEH WITH NON-CARVED, UNHEWN STONES." Yahweh is another Hebrew name for God.

The Book of Jeremiah is clear about the opinion of God concerning the monuments of the Satanists. Jeremiah 43:13 says: "HE SHALL BREAK THE OBELISKS OF THE TEMPLE OF THE SUN, IN EGYPT, AND WILL BURN THE TEMPLES OF EGYPT," including the most fascinating temples of Egypt, the pyramids. The George Washington Monument is an obelisk; we will see the reason for this in another chapter.

God rejects the sculptures of carved stone like the pagan statues symbolizing beast-men and the Egyptian sphinxes. In some American pyramids, we can see on the exterior sculpture and drawings of horrible serpents (the symbol of Satan). Regarding this, God says in Exodus 20:3 and 4: "You shall have no other gods before me. DO NOT MAKE CARVED IMAGES." Exodus 20:23–26 says: "You shall not make gods of silver alongside me, nor gods made of gold. YOU WILL MAKE AN ALTAR OF STONE . . . AND IF YOU MAKE AN ALTAR OF STONE, DO NOT DO IT OF CARVED STONES . . . and besides you shall not go up by steps to my altar," as people

16

used to do in pyramids, which have stairs to reach the top where millions of human sacrifices were carried out to honor Satan.

Numbers 33:53 says that when the sons of Israel arrived in Canaan, they had to "destroy all of the sculpture and all of the cast images, and demolish all their high places." Deuteronomy 4:16 says: "Do not corrupt yourselves, making carved images," and Deuteronomy 7:25 says: "You shall burn by fire the carved images of their gods; . . . because this is an abomination to Yahweh." Deuteronomy 12:2 and 3 say: "You will totally destroy all the places where the people who you are about to dispossess worship their gods. On the mountain heights, on the hills, and under every leaf tree; break down their altars, their pillars, burn their carved images and their gods and make their names disappear from their memory." Ezekiel 20:32 mentioned that the Israelites say: "We will be like the nations, like the nations of the earth, worshiping wood and stone." "The stone" occupied a good part of the thinking of the pagan. To the Satanists the stone was the material to build pyramids and temples; some stones, like the angular stone and the first or fundamental stone, were places where the pagans used to make human sacrifice as part of the satanic "mysteries." To the Christians, "the stone" is Jesus Christ, the one opposed to human sacrifice and pyramids.

Psalm 78:58 (not a psalm by David) says: "they provoke him to anger with their high places and their sculptures"; they provoke God with their sculptures of beast-men, serpents, and other idols. (We will see later that a number of Psalms are satanic). Joshua 8:31 says that Joshua made an altar to Yahweh on Mount Ebal according to: "what was written in the book of the Law of Moses; AN ALTAR OF NON-CARVED STONES, ON WHICH NO IRON TOOL HAS BEEN USED." There is no doubt about the rejection by God of the pyramids, which are monuments built of "carved stones." The follower of God never built pyramids. They made altars of non-carved stones.

Deuteronomy 27:15 says: "Cursed are those who make sculptures or cast images . . . and put them in hidden places." All the ancient civilizations made statues and other sculptures made of carved stones to honor "gods," to honor "idols," which means to honor demons. Jeremiah 3:9 says: "And contaminated the earth with their fornications, committing adultery with the stone and the wood." Habakkuk 2:19 says: "Woe to those who say to the wood: Wake up and to the stone: Stand up."

The Koran, like the Bible, is clear concerning the fact that the pyramids were monuments made by pagans. According to the Koran 17:92 and 95, the unbelievers had said: "we will not believe you at least you have a house adorned with golden or YOU GO TO HEAVEN BY USING STAIRS . . . " which means, with a pyramid, which is considered by the Satanists as a stair to reach heaven. The Koran continues saying in Sura 26:129: "You will raise buildings, apparently TO LIVE IN THEM ETERNALLY?" It refers to the pyramids, which are tombs for the Pharaohs and pre-Columbian Indian rulers who thought that they would live forever their false immortality. Other verses in the Koran, which speaks about pyramids without mention of the word "pyramid" are: 6:35; 28:38; 40:38 and 39; 52:38; and 70:3 and 4. Muhammad says this because he knew very well the satanism, not because he rejected it; we will see this in other chapters. God rejected the making of carved stones. This was not due to the stones per se, but because the temples built with carved stones were dedicated to the devil. In those temples, human sacrifices were made to honor the serpent; it is good to remember what the "stone of sacrifice" was in Mexico, it was a carved stone dedicated to the "goddess" Coatlicue: It was a kind of altar made of carved stones, in which there were sculpted serpents, and in this altar the Indians committed human sacrifice.

The God of Abraham was opposed to the building of temples because those constructions were typical of pagans, and

God wanted the human beings to distance themselves from the criminal pagans. For this reason the followers of God built altars different from those of the pagans. Other examples are the following verses: Genesis 28:18 and 22 say: "Jacob woke up very early, and he took the stone that he had as a pillow, and he put it as a memorial, and put oil on top of it, and then he said: This stone that I have put as a memorial will be a house of God for me." Genesis 31:45, 46, 51 and 52, and Genesis 35:14 describe something similar.

Exodus 24:4 says that Moses: "Woke up in the morning, and built an altar at the foot of the mountain and set up twelve stones." In Exodus 25, 26 and 27, God ordered Moses to make an altar in which he was to use wood, metal, and cloth; he did not order him to make it of carved stone. Deuteronomy 27:2–6 also speak of the construction of an altar that was later made by Joshua, according to the Book of Joshua 4:1–9 and 19 and 20 in which Yahweh said to Joshua: "Choose from among the people, twelve men . . . take twelve stones, bring them and put them in the place you will camp tonight," and Joshua said that: "those stones will be forever a memorial for the son of Israel."

Joshua 8:29 says that he put "a group of stones" over the dead body of King Hai, who was defeated by Joshua. Joshua 22:9–28 says: "the son of Ruben, the son of Gad and the half tribe of Manasses built an altar at the edge of the River Jordan, a very big altar"; the rest of the sons of Israel decided "to make war with them" for making "AN ALTAR DIFFERENT FROM THE ALTAR OF YAHWEH," but they went there and saw "the shape of the altar" and noticed that the altar was not different from the altar dedicated to God. These verses clearly indicate that the Israelites knew that they could not build altars similar to those of the pagans. Joshua 24:25–28 says of other occasions on which Joshua takes a big stone and says: "This stone will be a testimony against you . . . so you do not reject our God." Judges 6:26 says: "Build with wood an altar to Yahweh, your God;" it did not say to make it of carved stones. First Samuel 6:14, 15, and 18, 7:12, and 14:33–35, also speak in a similar way about the order of God to build monuments of noncarved stones.

First Kings 18:31 and 32 say about the leader of the prophets (Elias, who was loved by Jesus Christ): "Elias took twelve stones . . . and built with them an altar in the name of Yahweh." Isaiah, another prophet loved by Jesus Christ, said the following about the pagan temple in 27:9. "Yahweh destroyed the stone of their altars." Oseas 8:14 says: "Israel forgot their maker and built palaces," and of Judah says: God "will devour their palaces." Saint Mark 15:46 says that after Jesus died, he was put "in a monument that was carved into the rock"; he was not put into a pyramid or a temple made of carved stone.

Other type of pagan constructions were the pillars; they were a group of tree trunks placed in a standing position that were used as an altar. Another type of altar was made of stones grouped together, sometimes above the place where a dead body was buried. The Bible has many verses against those constructions. For example: Exodus 23:24: "Do not worship their gods, do not imitate their customs, and destroy their stone altars." Exodus 34:13 says: "Destroy their altars, break down their stone altars and destroy their pillars." Other verses that speak against the satanic practice of building stone altars and pillars are: Deuteronomy 7:5, 12:3, 16:21 and 22; Judges 3:7, 6:25:1 Kings 14:23, 15:13, 16:33, 2 Kings 3:2, 10:26 and 27; 13:6, 17:10, and 18:4.

Another pagan altar is called "high places" in the following books. Leviticus 26:30: "I will destroy your high places; I WILL DESTROY YOUR ALTARS CONSECRATED TO THE SUN." First Kings 11:7 and 8 say: "Solomon built in the mountain that is in front of Jerusalem a high place to Camos, an abomination of Moab." Other verses concerning the same topic are Genesis 49:26, Numbers 33:53, 1 Samuel 9:12–14.

There are dozens of biblical verses against the building of pagan temples and altars. The fighting in the Bible against the construction of satanic temples occupies an important place. The struggle was not a secondary issue, it was vital; for this reason there are abundant verses against those temples. The pyramids were the most noticeable temples of some ancient nations; at the top of them millions of humans were sacrificed to honor the devil in violation of the primary precepts, which say: "You shall not kill."

4. Worshipers of the Serpent

Almost every nation had myths about superhuman beings represented by a serpent. This was not a coincidence. All those peoples were part of a single united and connected entity ruled by Satan (and he is called serpent). In Egypt, Babylon, India, America (Mexico and Central America), people knew that the worship of the serpent was part of the religion that also built pyramids and made human sacrifices. It is possible that some people of those nations did not know exactly who the serpent was, but the priests, kings, and "initiated" knew perfectly the identity of the serpent. One of the attributes of the "serpent god" is: to provide "wisdom" and knowledge, useful for making "civilized" nations (including the teaching of human sacrifice and other perversions).

In Egypt the Pharaoh carried on the forehead an image of a serpent and some of their gods were represented by serpents. In America, temples and pyramids were full of drawn and sculpted serpents, and one of his main gods (Quetzalcoatl) was represented by a serpent. The serpents in the forehead of the Pharaoh and the god Quetzalcoatl were accompanied by the head of a bird (in the forehead of the Pharaoh) and by spread wings in Quetzalcoatl. Because it was a serpent with plumes, they called it the Plumed Serpent (or Winged-Serpent). The main god of the Mayan was KuKulKan, the Plumed Serpent. On the forehead of the Pharaoh was the image of a bird, but the concept is the same in all nations: SERPENT AND A BIRD IN THE SAME SYMBOL, THE SYMBOL OF SATAN. In

China, the "Dragon" (a reptile or a serpent with wings) influenced several aspects of daily life, and some others gods were represented by a serpent. In India, the serpent was a symbol of magical power and some gods were represented by a serpent. The same thing happened in almost every ancient nation.

Some scholars say that Satan was a creation of the human mentality as a product of the fear caused to them by beasts and natural phenomena in prehistorical time. They say that this emotion of fear was strongly established in the limbic area of the cerebrum, and from there, nerve impulses were sent to certain cortical areas of the cerebrum, which then turned the emotion of fear into an idea that implicates the belief in something "bad and invisible" existing out of our mind. This cerebral area called the limbic area has been called the "R" area, which is the first letter of the word "reptile" (this area is also called reptilian area); the name is very suspicious and suggestive because we already know that the "reptile" called serpent came to earth to teach us how to kill our own children and siblings, as Cain did to Abel instigated by the Serpent (the serpent is a reptile; when talking about Satan it has to be written with capital "S"); it is precisely in this limbic area that we find the cerebral structure related with violence and aggression. The Satanists want to keep this limbic area very active and alive, because it produces violence, whereas the followers of God and Christ want to atrophy this area through the practice of a Christian life.

Some perverse and ignorant say that Satan was the creation of the ancient Israelite and Christians. These are lies destined to cover up those who today are Satan's followers, including those who today are the "masters" of the world: the Jewish-Masonic organization. They know very well that Satan is a real and objective entity who came to earth, appeared to the Sumerians, and taught them all of the diabolic and devilish perversions. The common people of the ancient nations did not choose the serpent as a symbol of evil. The belief in Satan and the use of the serpent as the symbol of Satan was imposed on them by the men of power (who were Satanists).

In Babylon there was a dragon considered to be a god; we read that in Daniel 14:23: "There was a dragon revered by the Babylonians." The Sumerians, the first civilization of the planet, had histories about serpents, for example, Lahmu and Sahamu were horrible serpents. In the Sumerian story called Gilgamesh, intervened a monstrous serpent. The god Enlil in Babylon used to be represented as a dragon with two horns. Also in Babylon there was a history about a king taken to heaven by an eagle that had been thrown into a pit by a serpent. Note in this last story the presence of a bird and a serpent. Bird and serpent together in a story, or sculpted or drawn in pyramid or pagan temples, was a manner of representation of Satan, the plumed serpent. In Rome the serpent was also worshiped as a god. In Rome a story says that some beings possessed the human at the moment of birth and that after death, the being appeared as a serpent. The nation of the Hittites had stories about a dragon called Illyanka. The Phoenicians were worshipers of the plumed serpent. Astarte, a Canaanite and Phoenician god, used to be represented by a serpent. The first Gnostics believed in the existence of a being half-man and half-serpent.

Ahura Mazda, the supreme god of Zoroastrianism, was also represented with a WINGED SOLAR DISC; this was composed of a circle that represented the sun-god, two serpents and two wings. In India the worship of the serpent was also fanatical. Vishnu, a Hindu god, is frequently represented riding an eagle and leaning on a serpent. The Buddha, the creator of Buddhism, was protected in the middle of a storm by Mucalinda (a serpent that was the king of the serpents) intertwined in the body of the Buddha. Buddha said that he received illumination while he was in a moment of contemplation under a tree and protected by a serpent; according to Genesis, in a tree the Serpent appeared to Eve and made her sin, disobeying God and following the devil. Notice that in the story of the Buddha, the serpent had a "positive" role, "illuminating" the Buddha. In Genesis, the serpent has a malignant role.

The Vedas, the sacred book of India, speaks about the god Ashi, who was represented by a serpent. In that same country, a religious festival called Sarpabal had as a principal goal or objective to worship the serpent as the god of rain. Also, in this country, a story says that some kings of Nagpur were descendants of Nagas, which were the spirits of serpents. The Medo-Persians knew about a serpent called Gokcin. Also in Iran (ancient Persia) there was a serpent-god called Azi-Dahaka. In Asia the Hadju-dajaks symbolized the sky by a bird and the earth by a serpent (notice that the bird and the serpent are together in another story of a pagan people).

The Nordic people also have stories about serpent-gods. For example the god Thor and the god Loki participated in stories together with serpents. In Scandinavia, Igrasil is a cosmic tree, which has an eagle on one branch, a cobra on another branch, a squirrel and a deer on other branches; at the root of the tree is the serpent Nidhogg: the eagle fights each day with the serpent in this story (notice once more the serpent and the eagle together). Also for these people the god Edda was a big serpent. In China there is a story about the monster Kung-Kung, which had the body of a serpent. Also in China there was a story about Tu-hi, one of the founders of the Chinese civilization, who was born in a pond full of dragons. In North America some tribes had a dance called "the dance of the serpent."

In Egypt some gods that were represented by a serpent were: Apofis, Edjo, Uto, Mentseger, Atum, Seth, and Renemutest. The god Nekhbet was represented by a vulture (a bird) and the god Edjo by a cobra. Together they form the "ureus," which was the symbol used by the Pharaoh on his forehead, as I said before (the serpent and bird as the main symbol of the

Pharaoh, the symbol of Satan). The god Atum used to be represented by the winged solar disc, which had a circle representing the sun god, two serpents on both sides of the circle, and two spread wings on both sides of the circle. These symbols (the winged solar disc and the winged serpent) were the most important used in Egypt; we can see these symbols in almost every pyramid and temple. The combination of the winged solar disc and the plumed serpent can be seen at the top of the cover of this book. The worship of the serpent dates back to before the construction of pyramids; the pyramid builders knew that they were building pyramids under the guidance of the criminal hand of the plumed serpent. (The eagle and serpent are essential parts of the symbolism of the governments of Mexico and the United States of America, nations created by the Satanist Freemasons; we will talk about this later in another chapter).

The sun was considered a god by all of the ancient nations. The sun was part of the winged solar disc of the Egyptians. This symbol seems to signify among other things, Satan traveling around the world teaching perversion to humans; other scholars think that the meaning is Satan, the plumed serpent, bringing wisdom and benefits from the sun-god to earth (we already saw that according to the biblical book Apocalypse, Satan deceived all the earth; he deceived humankind at the time of giving "wisdom"). Besides, the sun-god is the provider of life according to the pagans. The winged solar disc has been found in all of the following nations: Egypt, Assyria, Persia, Phoenicia, and America. In America, Huitzilopochtli (a god of the Aztecs) took the Indian from a place called "Aztlan" to their final destiny in Mexico. This god told the Indian that the final destiny would end when they see an eagle in a tree eating a serpent. Note once again an eagle and a serpent together in a story. This story is symbolized in the Mexican flag. The Mayan goddess Cvacoatl was a serpent-goddess. The ensign of Tlaloc, the Mexican rain god, is formed by the intertwining of two serpents. The Mayan

26

and Aztec pyramids are profusely decorated with sculptures and drawings of serpents. The worship of serpents was fanatical in America.

❧   ❧   ❧

While all the ancient nations worshiped the serpent, the Christians rejected it and considered it an enemy of God and the human race. There are abundant biblical verses against the serpent. Those who did not believe in the Bible in 1492 should be surprised when the "conquistadores" discovered an ample continent in which the main gods were represented by serpents, exactly as the Bible described. Those American people who worship the serpent also committed human sacrifices, ate the flesh of the sacrificed, and also knew astronomy and practiced astrology. All these things are forbidden in the Bible.

The following biblical verses speak against the serpent: In Genesis 3:14 and 15, we see that after Satan deceived the humans and taught them a wisdom that did not come from God, this said: "Cursed are you among all animals, the human being will strike your head, and I will put enmity between you and the woman." Leviticus 11:41 and 44 say: "It will be for you an abomination every reptile on the earth," and also says "sanctify yourselves and be holy, for I am holy, you will not defile yourself with reptiles of the earth." Deuteronomy 8:14 and 15 say: "Do not forget Yahweh, your God who took you out from the land of Egypt, from the house of slavery, and led you through the great and horrible desert of serpents of fire." Deuteronomy 32:17 and 33 say: "They sacrifice to demons, to non-gods", and about those sacrificers, the Bible adds that their "wine is the poison of dragons, mortal poison of asps" (asps are a kind of serpent). The rejection by God of the serpent is clear in 2 Kings 18:4 in which it is said what the Jewish King Ezequias did to the serpent called Nejustan.

This serpent was made by the Israelites in a moment of disobedience and sin; the verse says: Ezequias "made high places disappear, broke the stone altars, threw down the pillars, and broke the bronze serpent that was made by Moses." Second Kings 21:6 says that Manasses, a king of Judah, sinned in the sight of Yahweh; "he made his son pass through fire; he was devoted to observing the clouds and serpents to obtain augury, and established mediums and wizards." We see here in a single verse the rejection of God to human sacrifices, to the serpent and to astrology, which are three of the main characteristics of the serpent empire. The Book of Esther in chapter 11 verse 5 and 6 speaks about two dragons that Mardoqueo saw in a dream: "He dreamed that he heard voices and noise, lightning bolts, earthquakes and great noise on earth when two big dragons, ready to fight each other, made a strong noise, and at the same time got ready to make war with all the nations of the earth in order to fight against the nation of the righteous." The concept of the dragon in this story means that these two nations were pagan nations.

The serpent is identified with evil in the Book of Job. In this book in a moment of pain, Job says of the night he was born: "Curse it, those who know how to curse the sea, those who know how to rouse up Leviathan"; you can read this in Job 3:8. Leviathan is another name of the serpent. (The Book of Job is one of the "books of wisdom" that has satanic teachings). Psalms 74:12–14 (not a Psalm of David) says: "God my King is from of old, working salvation in the earth. With your power you divided the sea and broke in the water the heads of the beasts. You crushed the heads of the Leviathan and you gave him as food for the marine monsters." In Genesis we saw that God advised the human to crush the head of the serpent. Psalm 89:11 (not a Psalm of David) says about God: "You crushed Rahab like a carcass"; it is said that Rahab is the primitive chaos and at the same time the serpent that tends toward chaos. Isaiah

28

51:9 says about God and his struggle against Satan: "Awake, awake, put on strength, the arm of Yahweh, awake, like in ancient time, in the remote centuries. Was it not you who crushed Rahab and pierced the dragon?" Psalm 58:5 says about the corrupt: "They have venom like the venom of serpents; they are deaf asps"; this Psalm is one of the Davidian Psalms, which means it was written by King David, or by one of his followers.

I mention this last Psalm here to show that the Satanists knew the identity of the serpent. Psalm 91:12 and 13 say that the righteous will be taken by angels "by their hands so they do not hit against the stones. Step on the asps and serpents, and trample the lion and the dragon." Psalm 140:4 (a Psalm of David) says about the sinner: "They made their tongue sharp as a serpent, they have under their lips serpents venom." Ecclesiasticus 21:2 says: "As from the serpent, run away from the sin." Ecclesiasticus is a satanic book, its author knew that the serpent is a malignant entity. (The Old Testament is divided into three sections: 1. the Law [the five books of Moses, which are the first five books of the Bible], 2. the Books of Wisdom, written by David, Solomon, and their followers [Job, Ecclesiastes, Ecclesiasticus, some Psalms, Proverbs, Wisdom, Lamentations, Song of Songs, and the historical books which focus on the Davidian messianism], and 3. the Prophets. Jesus Christ only approved "the Law and the Prophets"). Isaiah 26:21 and 27:1 say: "The Lord will come out from his place to punish the iniquity of the inhabitants of the earth. . . . That day Yahweh will punish with his heavy sword, big and powerful, the Leviathan, the fleeing serpent; the Leviathan, the twisting serpent, and he will kill the dragon that is in the sea."

Isaiah knew that the plumed serpent was also called Satan and knew that the religion of the serpent was the religion of Egypt. For this reason Isaiah says in 30:2 and 6, and in 34:14 and 15: "They take the road to Egypt without consulting me, to ask for help from the Pharaoh, and to seek shelter in the shadow of Egypt, . . . They harnessed the beast of burden to go south through a deserted region from which the lion and lioness, the viper and the FLYING DRAGON come." In Egypt where the Satanists lived "the nocturnal demons will have their dwelling, . . . There the serpent will make his nest." The "flying dragon" is the same "plumed serpent," the serpent that has plumes for flying. Isaiah also mentions the flying dragon in chapter 14 verse 29. About the serpent-god of Egypt and other gods, Exodus 12:12 says that God "will punish all the gods of Egypt." In Ezekiel 8:10, we see that during a period of corruption of the Israelites (which was the rule) there was in the Temple of Jerusalem: "every kind of image of reptiles and abominable beasts and all the idols of the house of Israel drawn on all around the walls."

In Mark 16:17 and 18, we read that Jesus Christ said: "In my name they will cast out demons, they will speak new tongues, they will take the serpent in your hand, and if they drink deadly things, they will not hurt them." In Matthew 3:7, Jesus Christ called the sinners: "race of vipers!" In Matthew 7:9 and 10, Jesus Christ says: "Is there anyone among you who if your child asked for bread will give him a stone, or if the child asked for a fish would give him a snake?" In this last verse, we see that Jesus Christ opposed the "stone" and the "serpent" (satanic concepts) to the "bread" and "fish" (positive concepts; the bread and the fish were symbols used later on by the first Christians).

In Matthew 23:33, we read that Jesus Christ called the rebel Israelites: "nest of serpents, race of vipers." The Book of Wisdom in chapter 12:24 and 27 says: "Many people deviated on the path of error, having for gods the most vile animals, deceived in a manner of foolish children, and they were punished by means of the same animals that they worshipped as gods." In this last verse, he is talking about the serpents that bit the rebel Israelites in the desert during the time of Moses, which was a reason for them to make a bronze serpent that cured the sick ones. This serpent was called the serpent of Najustan. This incident is clarified also in chapter 16:5, 6, 7, and 10, which says: "When the terrible rage of the beasts came upon them and they died by the bite of the twisting serpents, your wrath did not continue to the end. They were a little bit troubled to correct them; they have a signal of health to make them remember the precepts of the law. THOSE WHO TURNED TO LOOK AT IT WERE NOT CURED BY THE THING THEY SAW, BUT FOR YOU, OUR SAVIOR. But your children were not conquered by the teeth of the venomous serpent, because your mercy helped them and cured them." This bronze serpent was later destroyed by the Jewish King Ezequias. I do not believe that these verses were written by King Solomon. This Book of Wisdom (called the Wisdom of Solomon) contains non-satanic verses that obviously were included in this book of wisdom. I will talk later about this topic.

The Book of Job in chapter 40 and 41 showed that Job knows the symbolism of the serpent and the dragon. In these chapters he talks about a crocodile that "from his mouth came flames and he could see everything from above. He is the king of all beasts." Job describes a crocodile (a reptile as the serpent) that threw fire from the mouth and that is in the sky (for which he needs wings). Clearly he is talking about the dragon, or the flying dragon, which is the same to say the plumed serpent, also called Satan and devil.

The winged solar disc is one of the main symbols of the satanic civilization that built pyramids and made human sacrifices. Many historians believe that this was the main symbol in ancient Egypt, I also believe so. This symbol is a representation of Satan. Sometimes it does not have the two serpents on both sides. The true follower of God knew the meaning of the pagan symbols. The following biblical verse clearly expresses God's rejection of the Egyptian religion. Because the winged solar disc (Satan) had brought only death since the time he came to earth, God condemned him and proposed that in contrast "A SUN OF JUSTICE WILL RISE UP, THAT WILL BRING HEALING ON HIS WINGS." This verse mentions sun and wings, which is a clear reference to the winged solar disc. This verse is written in Malachi 4:2.

We should learn now what a volute is. A volute is a drawing, sculpture, or carved image that we can see very frequently on walls and columns of temples and pyramids. This symbol has the form of a SPIRAL line. This volute is a subliminal representation of a coiled serpent. Because the worship of the serpent was fanatical in the ancient civilizations, the use of the volute was also fanatical. Not only in ancient times, but also in modern times. Many of big edifices in Europe and North America (mainly those that were built several decades ago) have as part of their structural adornments carved volutes. Frequently they are on the frieze above the main entrance door on those edifices. Another symbol that you can see frequently on the frieze is the winged solar disc, sometimes modified with two branches on both sides of the circle instead of two serpents. Every leaf of the branch represents a feather of the wing of the winged solar disc; the circle represents the sun.

In these mentioned verses we saw that the Bible knows that the ancient people worshiped the serpent or the dragon. There are more biblical verses on the serpent that for reason of space I have not mentioned or analyzed.

5. Human Sacrifices in the Serpent's Empire: Satan, Murderer since the Beginning

Human sacrifice, committed by almost all of the ancient nations, was the characteristic that clearly indicated that those nations were guided by a malignant entity. If Satan was a human invention produced by the fear of beasts and natural phenomena, why did the cortical cerebral area try to appease the limbic area to eliminate the emotion of fear teaching the people to make human sacrifice? This theory about the origin of Satan is nonsense. The devil was not created by our minds, he exists outside of our minds. Some scholars believe that a group of Sumerian priests (in the first civilization of the world) created this idea: the idea that Satan could give long life, benefits, power, and bountiful harvests to the people. In exchange Satan requested the blood of human sacrifice.

In India, human sacrifices were committed. In the valley of Brahmaputra, the tribe Chota Naga made human sacrifices to guarantee plentiful harvests. The Gondos tribe of the same country sacrificed humans during planting and harvesting times. Besides, in India during funerary rites, they burned alive the widow of the deceased husband. In China and Japan, the people also made human sacrifices. In Canaan and Phoenicia, the same thing occurred. The Phoenicians particularly liked to sacrifice children. In Mindanao, a Philippine island, human sacrifices were committed. The "civilized" Greeks made human sacrifices during the festivals to honor the goddess Artemis and the god

Dionysus; these human sacrifices were opposed by Licurgo, the famous Greek philosopher.

In Egypt, women were sacrificed to honor the god Osiris. The Pharaohs sacrificed prisoners of war in temples adorned with serpents. The Pharaoh Amenhotep II (1427–1400 B.C.) practiced this and he wrote about it on a wall of a temple of Karnak. In Egypt thousands of human sacrifices were committed annually. This practice is testified to in a good number of walls of temples on which there are carved scenes of Pharaohs (for a period of approximately three thousand years) grasping with the left hand the hairs of a person's head and in the right lifted hand, the Pharaoh has a knife to decapitate the victim, and in front of the Pharaoh and the sacrificed are the images of the "gods" to whom the sacrifice was dedicated. Flavius Josephus, a famous Jewish historian of the first century of the Christian era, wrote of human sacrifice committed by the Egyptians in his book *Antiquities of the Jewish: Flavius Josephus Against Apion,* book 2 section 14: "Nevertheless Apion accuses us of sacrificing animals . . . And about the killing of domestic animals for sacrifice is a common thing for us and for all the men, but Apion when saying that it is a crime to sacrifice them, showed that he is an Egyptian himself, . . . But if all of the men followed the Egyptian custom, certainly THE WORLD WOULD BE DEPOPULATED OF HUMANS, but would be full of the most wild of THE BRUTE BEASTS, which BECAUSE THEY SUPPOSED THEY WERE GODS, they feed them carefully," and do not sacrifice those animals. But they did sacrifice humans to the demons to the point that they would lay waste the lands of humans. Josephus continues, saying that the Egyptians were dedicated "to the worship of gods, and to the study of the wisdom and philosophy" and that other "Egyptians assisted them in the killing of those sacrificed that they offered to the gods." Clearly Josephus is talking about human sacrifices because the Egyptians did not sacrifice animals.

In pre-Columbian America, there were temples with the same carved images that we can see in ancient Egypt: Indian rulers, taking by the hairs of the head one or several sacrificed to the gods; the posture of the body of the Pharaohs and the Indian rulers is the same: the right hand is raised, holding the knife with which they will kill the victims and the left hand at the level of the wrist, holding by the hairs the head of the victims. The posture of the sacrificed is also the same in Egypt and America: the victims are kneeling and the two inferior extremities are separated. This is not a coincidence; the Phoenicians brought from the Old World to America the practice of human sacrifices and the same manner of representing them in carved images. This image of the Pharaoh with the raised right hand and the left hand next to the wrist when sacrificing a victim has become a secret symbol used by Satanists in every continent and nation: Hitler, Lenin, Popes, Napoleon, etc., adopted this body posture in public acts.

The Egyptians sacrificed prisoners of war in the manner that I said. The same thing was done by the American Indians during war called *"Guerras Floridas"* (Florid Wars); they took prisoners of war to sacrifice them at the top of pyramids. The Narmer pallette is a piece of stone that depicts a Pharaoh of approximately 5,000 years ago, decapitating prisoners as an offering to a god. At this point, the readers should start understanding the reason why there is a pyramid drawn on the one-dollar bill: the founders of USA were followers of the religion that built pyramids and made human sacrifices on top of pyramids.

Pre-Columbian Amerindians made human sacrifices when sowing and harvesting. The Amerindians called Toltecs, Olmecs, Incas, Aztecs, and Mayans made horrible human sacrifices. There are reports that in one occasion the Aztecs sacrificed in few days about 8,000 humans (others say 80,000) during the inauguration of a temple dedicated to the "god"

Huitzilopochtli. The Aztecs also committed ritual cannibalism: they used to eat the flesh of those who were sacrificed at the top of pyramids. Some Aztec priests took the skin of victims in toto and put them on as a cloth during the cannibalistic ceremony. South American Indians had well-known Satanists called "decapitators"; these were priests or king-priests who sacrificed humans and were represented with the classical Egyptian-American manner: the sacrificers had a knife in the right hands and the left hands, grasping by the hairs of the head (sometimes already decapitated) of the victims.

It is almost incredible that in modern times there are people who adore the pyramids, even knowing that terrible and monstrous human sacrifices were always associated with pyramid building. A person has to be possessed by the Devil in order to open the chest of a live person with a knife and take the still beating heart out of the chest, as the Aztecs used to do. At the time the first pyramid of the world was built in Sumer, the rulers already had years of doing human sacrifice. The construction of pyramids and the human sacrifices are sine qua non of the religion of Satan; they always are together as an intrinsic aspect of the religion of the Serpent. The "Supreme Being" (the "Great Architect of the Universe," Satan), which is the "god" of the Freemasons, designed and built all the pyramids of the world, and also taught the humans to make human sacrifices in those pyramids.

Another pagan practice was to make an incision on their own body during religious ceremonies, with the purpose of shedding blood to give it to Satan as an offering. For instance, the Aztecs and Mayans used to pierce the ears, the tongues, and the penis to extract blood and offer it to the gods. The Hittites, Canaanites, Romans, and possibly, the Egyptians used to make body incisions with the same purpose.

These abominations and crimes were fought by the Bible (including the Law and the Prophets). God said the following in Leviticus 19:28: "Don't make incision in your body." Deuteronomy 14:1 repeats the same law. 1 Kings 18:28 said that the pagans: "cut themselves with knives, according to their custom, to the point of bleeding over them." Oseas 7:14 says: "They don't invoke me from the heart . . . they gash themselves for grain and wine and for these they make incisions." The oath of the "patriots" who made the "independence" of the Dominican Republic was sealed with blood that they took from some of their fingers; the oath was made at the same time that they invoked a religious entity: the Virgin Mary; they made incisions on their fingers in clear violation of the same book they draw in the national flag and shield: the Bible. The leader of those "patriots" was Juan Pablo Duarte, a Mason. It is believed that other "patriots" participants in that oath were also Masons.

The following biblical verses are clear concerning the rejection by God of the human sacrifices. Exodus 20:13: "You shall not murder." Matthew 5:21 and Mark 10:19 narrate that Jesus Christ quoted the Law and said: "You shall not murder." Psalm 106:28, 36, 37 and 38 (not a Psalm of David) says: "They worshipped Baalfogor and ate the sacrifice of dead gods and worshipped their idols and SACRIFICED THEIR OWN SONS AND DAUGHTERS TO DEMONS; THEY SHED INNOCENT BLOOD, THE BLOOD OF THEIR SONS AND DAUGHTERS, SACRIFICING THEM TO THE IDOLS OF CANAAN."

The Bible speaks against the custom of eating the flesh of the sacrificed as the pagans of the Old World and America used to do. The Book of Wisdom 12:3–6 says: "They practice horrible works of magic, impious rites," and "THEY WERE CRUEL ASSASSINS OF THEIR CHILDREN, AND THEY HAVE BANQUETS WITH HUMAN FLESH AND BLOOD, and with the blood, they participate in infamous orgies. To those fathers, ASSASSINS OF INNOCENT BEINGS, YOU DETERMINED TO DESTROY THEM BY THE HANDS OF

OUR ANCESTORS." (The Book of Wisdom is in reality two books in one, the first eleven chapters are satanic, the rest are not satanic).

Ezekiel 20:31 says that the sinners "MAKE YOUR CHILDREN PASS THROUGH THE FIRE, YOU CONTAMINATE YOURSELVES WITH IDOLS." Ezekiel 23:37 also says "THEY COMMITTED ADULTERY WITH THEIR IDOLS, AND EVEN THE CHILDREN THEY HAD BORNE TO ME PASSED THEM THROUGH FIRE AS A FOOD OFFERING" to the gods.

Jesus Christ says about Satan: "HE IS A MURDERER SINCE THE BEGINNING" (Saint John 8:44). Leviticus 18:21 says: "You will not give your son as an offering to Moloch" (Moloch was a god of the Ammonites). Ajaz, a Jewish king of Judah who was a Satanist, "passed his son through the fire, according to the abomination of those people that Yahweh had expelled in front of the son of Israel" (2 Kings 16:3).

Second Kings 17:17 says: "THEY PASSED THROUGH THE FIRE THEIR SONS AND DAUGHTERS, THEY PRACTICED DIVINATION AND ENCHANTMENT." Second Kings 17:31 says: "THEY PASSED THEIR CHILDREN THROUGH THE FIRE, TO HONOR ADRAMELEC AND ANAMELEC, GODS OF SEFARVAIM." Second Chronicles 33:1–17 say: that Manasses the king of Judah, "sinned before the eye of Yahweh" because "he raised up altars to the Baals, he made pillars and worshipped all of the legions of the sky"; besides, "he raised up altars in the house of Yahweh ... to honor all the legions of the sky" and "PASSED HIS CHILDREN THROUGH THE FIRE IN THE VALLEY OF BEN-HINNON; he studied the dreams, practiced magic, having with him magicians" and made "a cast statue in the house of God." (The Bible condemnations in the former, in this paragraph and next lines, are against the Jews). In this last chapter, we see a condemnation of human sacrifice and astrology. The Book of

Wisdom 14:23 says that God rejected the Satanists because they "celebrate initiation rites and commit INFANTICIDE, or OCCULT MYSTERIES, and strange rites." Today there are secret societies that practice "mystery" rites and adore the religion of pyramids and human sacrifices. Freemasonry is one of those societies. For this reason they drew a pyramid on the dollar bill.

Isaiah, the prophet beloved by Jesus, says in 57:3–5: "Come here, you, children of sorcerers, you offspring of an adulterer and a whore. Whom are you mocking? Against whom do you open your mouth wide and stick out your tongue? Are you not children of sin, offspring of lies, you that burn with lust among the oaks and under every green tree. SACRIFICING CHILDREN IN THE VALLEYS, UNDER THE CLIFFS OF THE ROCKS?"

Not even animal sacrifices were requested by God, as we read in Jeremiah 7:21 and 22 where he says: "THUS SAYS YAHWEH SEBAOT, THE GOD OF ISRAEL: INCREASE THE NUMBER OF YOUR SACRIFICES AND EAT THE FLESH OF THE VICTIMS, WHEN I TOOK YOUR FATHERS FROM EGYPT I DID NOT TALK ABOUT HOLOCAUST AND SACRIFICES AND DID NOT ORDER THEM TO DO THAT."

Jeremiah 19:4 and 5 say that God will punish the sinner Israelites: Because the people "have forsaken me and have profaned this place, by offering incense in this place to strange gods whom neither they nor their ancestors nor the kings of Judah have known, FILLING THIS PLACE WITH THE BLOOD OF THE INNOCENT and building the high places of Baal, WHERE THEY BURN WITH FIRE THEIR CHILDREN AS HOLOCAUST TO BAAL." Baruch 4:7 says: "For you provoke the one who made you, SACRIFICING TO DEMONS, TO NON-GODS." Deuteronomy 32:17 says: "They sacrifice to demons, to non-gods." Second Kings 21:6 says about Manesses, the king of Judah, that I already mentioned: "HE

MADE HIS SON PASS THROUGH FIRE; HE OBSERVED THE CLOUDS AND THE SERPENTS TO GET AUGURY, AND TO ESTABLISH MEDIUMS AND SOOTHSAYERS." This verse speaks against three of the main characteristics of the serpent empire: human sacrifice, worship of the serpent, and astrology. First Kings 16:34 narrates that a Jew "rebuilt Jericho; he laid the foundation at the price of his firstborn, Abiram, and set up the gates at the price of Segub, his youngest son"; this is an ancient orthodox satanic practice: to make a human sacrifice at the time of setting up the first stone of a construction.

One of the biggest abominations that was committed by ancient nations were human sacrifices. They did it since remote time, following the teaching of Satan. The true God wanted the nations not to practice that, and in order to convince us not to do it, he sent prophets. The story of Abraham and the attempt to sacrifice his son was a teaching against human sacrifice. God asked Abraham to sacrifice his son and he innocently and obediently was ready to do it, but before doing that, God stopped him and told him to sacrifice an animal instead of his son. It was a very practical manner of saying: I do not want human sacrifice.

Previously, I analyzed a biblical verse in which God did not even ask for animal sacrifice, but rather obedience to the law. This was corroborated by Jesus Christ when during the Last Supper they only had wine and bread, they did not eat flesh from sacrificed animals. The devilish minds of all the actual Satanists, including the Freemasons, have deviated the meaning of these two teachings coming from God and Jesus. Those Satanists say that God really asked Abraham to sacrifice his son because God was one of the gods of the ancient nations who requested human sacrifices.

And about Jesus Christ, those buffoons say that during the modern church ceremony simulating the Last Supper of Jesus Christ, he (Jesus) actually appeared in person (in flesh) and therefore, the churchgoers are literally eating the blood and body of Jesus Christ. The Vatican called this phenomenon transubstantiation (transmutation) of the body and blood of Jesus Christ. This is a subtle and subliminal way of introducing secretly in our minds the idea that human sacrifice is a good thing to do because even Jesus Christ offered his body for a sacrifice.

Other Satanists say that Jesus Christ was a member of the serpent empire because he committed a self-sacrifice in order to bring benefits to humanity, as the pagans used to do, who at the top of pyramids sacrificed humans in order to reward the people with abundant harvests, a military victory, or to increase and make the power of the rulers stronger. It was an interchange between the gods and the humans: the rulers offered human sacrifices, and the gods paid back with benefits. But the Satanists do not mention that Jesus Christ and the Bible broke on their own faces their devilish theory when they rejected human sacrifice. (In any event, it is not necessary to argue and debate with Satanists about the purity of our Christian religion because they know perfectly that Satan is a murderer, but they prefer to follow the Devil because that is the inclination of their minds and their hearts.)

In order to keep alive and to receive benefits from the gods, the followers of Satan made human sacrifices. For the Christian, life is kept following these two commandments: You shall not kill, and you shall love one another.

6. Astrology and Spiritualism in the Serpent's Empire

It is not a secret that in the ancient nations where pyramids are found there was also knowledge of astronomy. The "illuminated" of the ancient civilizations believed in the existence and the use of a magnetic current that went throughout the universe and around the earth, and that this current influenced the body, the soul, and the behavior of humans. Some believed that the megaliths, pyramids, temples, and other structures were built following the geographic coordinates by which this magnetic force runs. Satanists call this magnetic force a spiritual force. The study of the movement of the stars was common to some ancient civilizations. They believed that human facts were related and predetermined by the cyclical appearances of stars and their movements.

From this idea astrology was born. Astrology subordinates the human will to the will of the stars, which the pagans considered as gods. But the Satanists deceived themselves because they offered destruction and death to those "gods" (the stars) that they say they keep the rhythm and life of the universe. Evidently they confused themselves. The reason for this is clear. According to Genesis, Satan came to earth and deceived Eve, offering her knowledge and wisdom, but at the same time, he requested human sacrifices, which prove clearly that Satan is not the true God of the harmonious universe, but the god of death, destruction, and loss of harmony among humans and the universe.

A clear proof of the practice of astronomy is the Zodiac of Dendera, in Egypt, which is a zodiac drawn on the ceiling of a temple. In pre-Columbian Mexico, the Aztecs had the "Calendar Stone," which was a big round stone with a carved zodiac. This is incontrovertible evidence that the Egyptians came to America approximately four thousand years ago.

There are a good number of biblical verses on the practice of astrology. I believe that the study of astronomy (and any other science) is not bad per se. It is a malignant activity when humans use it to increase ignorance and perversions. For instance, the ancient pagans waited for the appearance of certain stars or celestial phenomena in order to make human sacrifices, for example during the new moon or an eclipse. God is opposed to the astrology, among other reasons, because there was an intrinsic association among astrology, human sacrifices, and the use of hallucinogenic drugs.

Exodus 22:17 says: "You shall not allow a female sorcerer to live," which expresses opposition to sorcery, a practice associated with astrology (the biblical author of this verse forgot to say that the advice of killing a person does not come from God). Another pagan activity was to have a meeting in order to contact spirits and demons. They do so during rites of "initiation" or ceremonies, called "mysteries." The pyramids, for example, were "stairs" to "reach the heavens" and to meet with the "gods," which means with demons. Leviticus 19:26 says: "Don't practice divination or magic," and in 19:31 says: "Don't ask for help from those who evoke the dead, or wizards, don't consult them, don't be defiled by them." Leviticus 20:6 says: "If someone asks of those who evoke the dead and wizards, prostituting themselves before them, I will turn against him and exterminate him from his people." Deuteronomy 4:19 says: "Looking at the sky, the sun, the moon, the stars, to the all the hosts of the sky, don't deceive yourselves, worshiping them." Deuteronomy 18:9–12 says: "Don't imitate the abominations of those nations, don't permit to be among you someone who passes through the fire their son or daughter, or practices divination, or magic, or consults with wizards, or spirits, or asks the dead. Whoever does these is an abomination before Yahweh, and precisely for those abominations, Yahweh, your God, is taking away from you those people." First Samuel 28:3 says: "Saul made disappear from that land all those who evoke the deads or wizards" (later, Saul sinned doing the same, according to chapter 28 of that book).

Second Kings 23:4–20 say that God rejected the altars of the pagans, the human sacrifices, the astrology, and the cult of demons. In that book, Josias, king of Judah, ordered: "to take out from the temple of Yahweh all the utensils made for Baal, for the pillars and all the stars of the sky, and burn them outside Jerusalem, in the valley of Cedron, and take the ash to Betel. He expelled the priests of the idols, which were established by the kings of Judah to burn perfumes in the high places, in the city of Judah, and on the outskirts of Jerusalem; to those who offered perfumes to Baal, the sun, the moon, TO THE ZODIAC AND TO ALL THE STARS OF THE SKY. He took the pillars out from the house of Yahweh, out of Jerusalem, to the Valley of Cedron, and burned the pillars there, turning them into ash, and had them thrown to the common sepulchre of the people"; he also "profaned the Tofet of the valley of the son of Hinon, TO AVOID SOMEONE PASSING THROUGH FIRE THEIR SON OR DAUGHTER TO HONOR MOLOCH."

Isaiah 47:13 speaks in the following manner of the fall of Babylon: "Let them come now, let them save you, those who make the charts of the sky and watch the stars and count the months, let them save you from what will happen to you." The verse 47:10 says of Babylon: "YOUR WISDOM AND YOUR SCIENCE DECEIVED YOU." Isaiah 65:3 and 4 narrate the answer of God to a plea of the sinner Israelite: you are "a people who provoke me to anger permanently, sacrificing in gardens and burning incense over bricks; a people who go to sit in tombs and SPEND THE NIGHT WATCHING THE STARS."

Jeremiah 10:2 says: "So speaks Yahweh: Don't get accustomed to the manner of the people; DON'T BE AFRAID OF THE CELESTIAL PHENOMENA THAT PRODUCE TERROR ON THEM." Jeremiah 27:9 and 10 say: "Don't listen to your prophets, to your wizards, to your dreamers, TO YOUR ASTROLOGISTS and to your wizards that say: the king of Babel will not conquer you; because they lie to you." Zephaniah 1-2, 4 and 5 say: "I will sweep away everything from the face of the earth, says Yahweh. . . . I will exterminate from this place the rests of Baal . . . AND TO THOSE WHO BOW DOWN ON THE ROOFS TO THE STARS OF THE SKY."

There are more verses in the Bible against astrology and magic, which indicate that the struggle against them is an important aspect of the followers of God. To subdue the free will of the human being to the influence of the stars or universal magnetic currents is to take away from humans a valuable gift: FREEDOM. The Bible says clearly that the stars are only useful for bringing the light, not the "light" (wisdom) of the Satanists, but the physical light. We cannot live in a world in which we have to consult the stars in order to get married, choose a profession, have children or put the head of the bed of our room toward the east or the west, as some Masons do. The stars don't move the humans; we move the stars. Faith in Jesus Christ moves mountains.

7. Drugs in the Serpent's Empire

Another well-known aspect of the ancient pagans is the use of drugs to produce altered mental states. The Incas used cocaine in their religious ceremonies. They used to make sacrifices of children to honor the sun-god; before sacrificing them, they numbed them with cocaine. The Mayans used a kind of tobacco to intoxicate themselves when they evoked the spirit of the dead. Some of the drugs used by the Mayans were balche, gongos, peyote, and dolvihqui. On the Asian continent, the use of opiates dates back to remote times. The pagans believed that the use of drugs produced altered mental states favorable to the activity of the demons in the body. Besides, they believed that during meditation they can reach the same state. The Buddhists (followers of Buddha, who was protected by the Serpent), believed that they can reach an altered mental state called "nirvana." The Aztecs used drugs during religious ceremonies, for example, when making human sacrifices. The use of peyote by the Amerindians is well known; the peyote contains a potent drug. COCAINE HAS BEEN FOUND IN EGYPTIAN MUMMIES; we have to know that cocaine is native to America. This is another clear evidence that the Egyptians came to America in pre-Columbian time.

The use of hallucinogenic drugs produces neurophysiologic reactions in the brain including a reaction related with the ocular globes. The person who is using the drug finds that his two eyes move horizontally and inward and the two visual fields meet in the center between the two eyebrows. At the same time, the person is said to have astral projection, or sees or hears demons. This phenomenon is what the Satanists call the opening of the third eye. A similar phenomenon happens to those who drink alcohol; they have cross sighting; they cannot focus with both eyes on one single object in front of them. The production of those altered mental states was one of the perversions that Satan taught to humans.

The people of Israel received from the messenger of the true God rules about mental and physical health, and they criticized the use of drugs. The biblical book Ezekiel 8:17 says: "Do you think it is a light thing to the house of Judah to do the abomination done in this place? They have filled the land with violence to provoke my anger? And they also take the branch ("zemora" in Spanish) to their noses." This "zemora" seems to be a kind of leaf with hallucinogen properties. This practice reminds one of a similar practice of the Caribbean Indian Tainos. Ezekiel 8:10 says that in that same place where the Israelites used "zemora" (the Temple of Solomon, which is the "Temple of Jerusalem"), they practiced other abominations, including the worship of Satan in the form of a reptile. The verse goes: "I went in and looked, and I saw every kind of image of reptiles and abominable beasts and all the idols of the house of Israel drawn all around on the walls."

Today the problem of drug use is worse than forty centuries ago, and there is not an effective program to eliminate this problem because all the governments of Europe and America are reviving the Serpent's Empire. They do not want to eliminate the use of drugs because it is part of the satanic religion, their religion.

8. Worshipers of the Sun-God

Many of the rulers of the ancient nations considered the sun as a "god," and they considered themselves as sons of the "sun-god." The sun-god was considered the giver of life by the Egyptians. The worship of the sun-god was one of the most important religious beliefs of those people. This happened in Egypt, Japan, Europe, the reign of the Incas, and also in Central America and Mexico. Temples, altars, and pyramids have drawn or carved images of the sun-god profusely. This sun-god had to be fed with human blood from human sacrifices in order for Satan to continue to provide benefits to the humans.

In Egypt several gods were represented with the winged solar disc. I have already explained that this symbol consisted of a circle, which represents the sun, two wings on both sides of the circle, and frequently it also has two serpents on both sides of the circle. Some Egyptian gods represented by the sun were Aten, Horus, Ra, and Osiris. The Egyptian obelisks were dedicated to the sun-god. In the Inca empire, the worship of the sun-god was the official religion. These Incas used to give cocaine to boys and girls before sacrificing them to honor the sun-god. People of ancient Mexico considered the sun as a god who possessed vital forces, and they called him Ipalnemohuani, and sacrificed humans, opening the chest and taking out the still beating heart to offer it to the sun-god. In Rome, Apollo was the sun-god.

There are many verses in the Bible condemning the "solar religion." Let us see some. Leviticus 26:30 says, "I will destroy your altar dedicated to the sun." Deuteronomy 4:19 says: "Do not "raise your eyes to the sky, to the sun . . . worshipping them." Second Kings 23:5 says: the sinners in Israel were expelled because they "offered perfumes to Baal and the sun." Verse 11 says: "He made the horses that the kings of Judah had dedicated to the sun disappear from the entrance of the house of Yahweh" and "he burned the chariots of the sun." Ezekiel 6:4 says: "Your altars will be destroyed, and also your solar altar will be destroyed."

The worship of the sun-god is very active in modern times as we will see.

9. The Meaning of the Concept of "Stone"

Most of the buildings and monuments of the ancient civilizations were basically made of stones. The stone signified for those people the "material" used to "construct" their religion of demons. For this reason the Bible identified the "builders" with the worshipers of Satan, and for this reason, God prohibited the Israelites from making monuments of polished or carved stone. It is well known that at the time of placing the first stone of a temple (called the foundation stone) the pagans committed human sacrifices, and in some corners (in which the first stone is called a cornerstone) human sacrifices were also made. For the followers of God, the "stone" symbolized the opposite; it symbolized that what the humans built must be made of the "stone" called Jesus Christ, which means with peace and not human sacrifices. For this reason the Bible called Jesus Christ the "cornerstone" and "foundation stone." Psalms 118:22 and 23 (not a Psalm of David) says the following about the Satanist builders of temples and pyramids: "The stone rejected by the builders has been put as a chief cornerstone.

"This is God's doing, it is marvelous in our eyes." Those builders and their "stones" are beloved by the Freemasons; for this reason the god of the Freemasons is the "Great Architect of the Universe," the builder of all the temples and pyramids where millions of humans were sacrificed. This great architect and his workers believe that they will reach heaven using their temples and their "stairs-pyramids." They ignore the fact that to reach heaven, there is only one way: "I am the way, the truth, and the life; no one goes to the father, but through me." These are words of Jesus Christ in Saint John 14:6. What is said in Psalms 118:22 and 23 can be read in other biblical verses.

Isaiah said the following in 8:14 and 15 about Jesus Christ: "He will be a stone of scandal and stumbling stone," and the sinners will "stumble, will fall and will be broken" if they strike against this unbreakable stone called Jesus Christ. Isaiah 28:16–18: "I have put in Zion for a foundation a stone, a tested stone, a precious cornerstone, a sure foundation. One who trusts shall not make haste. And I will make justice the line and righteousness the plummet. . . . YOUR COVENANT WITH DEATH WILL BE BROKEN."

Stone, compass, and square are Masonic symbols: line, plummet, compass, square, rule and level are tools used by the "builders"; the Masons chose the compass and the square as some of their more important symbols. The Masons know that the Bible criticized these tools and that the Bible proposed to change the "line" and the "plummet" for "justice" and "righteousness." But the Masons chose the tool of the "builders" to make temples and pyramids and human sacrifices. Isaiah 34:11, speaking about a sinner city, says: "Yahweh will put on it the line of confusion and the plummet of emptiness." Isaiah 44:13 says about those who make idols to adore demons: "Another work with wood, take his measure with the line and make his mark with red ocher. He handles the plane and MARKS WITH THE COMPASS." First Peter 2:4, 5, 7 and 8 say about Jesus: "Come to him, as a living stone rejected by men, but chosen by God, a precious stone. You, as living stones, are built in spiritual house and holy priesthood to offer spiritual sacrifices, acceptable to God through Jesus Christ" and Jesus is "a stone rejected by the builders, and made cornerstone."

Jesus Christ also condemned this concept of stones and temples, according to Mark 13:1 and 2, which say: "Upon leaving Jesus Christ, the temple, one of the disciples told him:

Teacher, look at that large stones and large buildings! And Jesus told him: Do you see these big constructions? Not one stone will be left here upon another, all will be destroyed." The temple of this story is the Temple of Jerusalem; therefore, we clearly see that Jesus rejected the Temple of Jerusalem (the Temple of Solomon), which is beloved even today by Jews, Muslims, and Masons. In some Masonic temples (lodges), there are shapeless stones that symbolize the "imperfect state of men before they acquire the knowledge and "wisdom" they teach. The stone is used by the Freemasons as a symbol of their beliefs. When a man has acquired wisdom, then he becomes a "polished stone." They use all this symbolism of the "stone" to cover up the real meaning of the stone: the stones are used to make pyramids and temples in which the Satanists made human sacrifices. In opposition, the Christian "stone" is Jesus Christ, the king of peace. The main altar of the "holy" Muslim temple at Mecca is a big polished black stone; the implication is clear.

To finish, let's read Psalm 89:27 (it is not a Psalm of David): "You are my father, my God, the rock of my salvation"; and Jesus Christ says in Matthew 16:18: "I say to you that you are Peter, and over this stone I will built my church, and the door of the inferno will not conquer it." For the Christians, the "stone" is God and Jesus Christ; for the Freemasons the "stone" is Satan and his teaching.

10. Other Biblical Verses on the Serpent's Empire

These are others verses of the Bible that show that the writers of that book knew about the existence of the Serpent's Empire and fought against it.

Isaiah 14:26: "Here is the resolution against all the earth, here is the hand stretched out against all the nations." Genesis 6:7 says: "I will exterminate the men that I made over the face of the earth," and we had the deluge. First John 5:19 says: "WE KNOW WE ARE FOLLOWERS OF GOD, WHILE THE WHOLE WORLD IS UNDER THE CONTROL OF THE DEVIL." Isaiah, 13:11 says: "I will punish the world by his crimes." In the following verses, we see that Satan had an empire: "the Devil took Jesus to a mountain and showed him all the reigns of the world and told Jesus: All these things I will give you if you love me." Jesus rejected the offer, these can be read in Matthew 4:8 and 9.

Isaiah 34:1–3 says: "Come to me and listen; listen to me all the nations; earth and every thing on you, listen to me, the world and every thing it produces. Yahweh is irritated against all the nations."

The ancient Serpent's Empire came to an end when the Spanish arrived in America to destroy the satanic societies that built pyramids, worshiped the Serpent, and made human sacrifices. But those Spanish forgot that the Bible says in Ezekiel 33:11: "For my life, says the Lord, Yahweh, I have no pleasure in the death of the wicked, but that the wicked turn from their ways and live." The Spanish committed horrible crimes in America.

But Satan's soldiers have been working secretly in the shadows in order to revive the ancient Serpent's Empire. And they are well advanced in their worldwide criminal conspiracy.

11. The Old and the New World, a Single Unified Entity

It is absolutely impossible to accept that the abundant "similarities" between the Old and the New World are coincidences. These are some of the hundreds of EQUAL things found in both worlds: pyramids; worship of the serpent-god; worship of the sun-god; astronomy; astrology; the zodiac; human sacrifices; the use of drugs in religious ceremonies; mummification; pyramids used as tombs of the rulers; multiple coffins, with one inside the others protecting the dead body of a ruler; the use as a symbol of the winged solar disc; the use as a symbol of the plumed serpent; statues of the rulers with the same body posture; the use of leopard skin by the priests; the use of feathers over the heads by the Amerindians and the Egyptian royal family; the use of cocaine (found in Egyptian mummies; cocaine is extracted from the coca leaf which was only found in America in pre-Columbian time); human sacrifice, consisting of the decapitation of the victims (Pharaohs and Amerindian rulers holding by the hairs the heads of the victims as seen on walls of Egyptians and Amerindians temples); equal funerary towers in Mediterranean islands and Peru; the deformity of the head of the Pharaoh Akhenaten and the same deformity of the head of some Mayans (probably caused by compressing the head laterally for a long period of time); the use of the same material for making rafts in Peru and ships in Egypt, etc.

This book is not about the similarities between the Old and the New World. It is a very simple and easy thing to understand that these are not similarities. The reason why some scholars don't accept this fact as a truth is that all the governments of the world are under the control of Satanists who believe and follow this religion of pyramids and human sacrifices. It is not convenient for them that the world knows that they are the same sacrificers of ancient times and followers of those who killed Jesus Christ. The Satanists take advantages of the ignorance of the world concerning the existence of the Serpent's followers behind the throne of every nation. The media, the savants and scholars of the Vatican, others persons with university diplomas, and "Men in Power," they all work to cover up the existence of this Jewish-Satanic-Masonic conspiracy, which is not a conspiracy anymore (since the eighteenth century); they are already in power.

Part Two

12. Satan in Modern Times

"Lucifer is the life, Lucifer is the divine breath which keeps life on earth, Satan is the angel who brings life, he is the eternal wisdom." These incredible and blasphemous words were written by a Mason in a book (*"Por el Mundo de la Masoneria,"* by Pompilio A. Brower, see Bibliography). It is not a secret that the Freemasons are Satanists and anti-Christians. Freemasonry is a secret society dedicated to doing "works of compassion" and to make "perfect" the human mind and behavior. That's what they say about themselves; another and different is the reality. There are Freemasons all over the world; they claim to be between 2 and 5 million. The temples where they meet are called lodges. In order to be initiated as a Mason, one has to believe and make an oath of obedience to the "Supreme Being" (the "Great Architect of the Universe," which is no one other than Satan). Many of the lodges have no windows in order to avoid spying, but mainly to create the impression of "mystery" concerning their beliefs and their lives, and also to create the impression that they are in possession of deep, very important, and "mysterious" knowledge and wisdom.

I am exposing in this book much of the "secret" knowledge they claim to be in possession of. Actually, few Masons know the secrets that I am revealing in this book (probably no more than one hundred Masons know about it). They say that they are a religion or a group open to all those who want to be members independently of their beliefs. They say that Christians, Muslims, Buddhists, atheists, etc., can be members of

Freemasonry. A high number of kings, princes, earls, government ministers, presidents, dictators, etc., have been Masons all over the world, since approximately three centuries ago. Today a high number of presidents, dictators, and other men in power are Masons. The Masons are the responsible for the erection of all the obelisks that we see almost in every nation of the modern world. They built the only two pyramids constructed in post-Columbian time: the pyramid-tomb of Lenin in Moscow, Russia, and the "Columbus-Lighthouse" (the tomb of Columbus, in Santo Domingo, the Dominican Republic). The fundamentals of Freemasonry were created by those Jews who left Egypt during the Exodus and made the golden bull (an Egyptian idol) on Mount Sinai and opposed Moses. They persisted in Israel where they used to do human sacrifices at the valley of Ben-Hinnon, are called in the Bible "Rebels," and were called by Jesus Christ a "race of vipers." They built the satanic Temple of Solomon and created the first eleven chapters of "the Book of Wisdom" included in the Bible.

Later they were scattered throughout the world and reappeared in A.D. 1119 as a visible, international and powerful institution called "The Knights Templars." This group was destroyed at the beginning of the fourteenth century, and reappeared in the sixteenth century with the name it still has today: Freemasonry. Therefore, Freemasonry is a creation of the Jewish-Satanists who learned the satanic Egyptian religion during the four hundred years that the Israelites lived in Egypt before the Exodus. Properly talking, Freemasonry is a symbiosis of the satanic Egyptian religion and Jewish Satanism. In a previous chapter, I already mentioned the condemnation by the prophets of the human sacrifices committed by Israelites in Israel.

King David and his son King Solomon are the spiritual leaders of the Freemasons. I will clearly prove in this book that these two kings were Satanists and that they are the two satanic beasts described in the last book of the Bible (the Book of

Apocalypse, also called Revelation). Most of the followers of "Judaism" are not Satanist, but they ignore the terrible reality hidden behind their beliefs. The same happens with the Christians: they ignore that "Saint Paul" and the Vatican are satanic entities. The same is happening with the Muslims; they ignore that Muhammad and the Koran are also two satanic entities.

In the next chapters, I am going to prove that David and Solomon are the two beasts described in the Apocalypse. This will be the first time in almost two thousand years that these secrets concerning the satanism of David, Solomon, "Saint Paul" and Muhammad are exposed to the public, to the world.

13. Solomon, the Satanic and Apocalyptic Beast 666

The Judaists (the followers of "Judaism") respect and worship the Temple of Solomon. They do so because they believe that God authorized or ordered the construction of that temple, and by the belief that his promoter David and his builder Solomon were holy men of God. This belief is false. To continue I will transcribe the biblical chapter that speaks about King David's decision to build the temple. The reader should note, that God never accepted and/or authorized David to build a temple.

Second Samuel 7:1–29 says:

> When the king was settled in his house and Yahweh had given him rest, protecting him from all his enemies around, the king said to the prophet Nathan: see now; I am living in a house of cedar, and the ark of God is in a tent. Nathan answered the king: Go, do all that you have in your heart, for Yahweh is with you. But that same night the word of Yahweh came to Nathan: Go and tell David, my servant: Thus says Yahweh: Are you the one to build a house for me to live in? Look, I have not lived in a house since the day I brought up the people of Israel from Egypt to this day, but I have been moving in a tent, in a tabernacle. Wherever I have moved with the people of Israel, did I ever speak a word with any of the tribal leaders of Israel, whom I commanded to shepherd my people Israel, saying, Why have you not built me a house of cedar? Tell David, my servant: Thus says Yahweh Sebaot: I took you from the pasture from behind the sheep to be prince of my people, Israel. I have been with

you wherever you went; I have exterminated before you all of your enemies, and I am making for you a great name, like the name of the great ones of the earth, settling my people, Israel and planting them in his place so that they may live in their own place and will not be disturbed anymore, and evil doers shall afflict them no more as before, since the day in which I appointed judges over my people, Israel, and I will give you rest from all your enemies.

Moreover, Yahweh declares to you that he will build a house to you; and when your days are fulfilled and you lie down with your ancestors, I will raise up your offspring after you, who shall come forth from your body, and I will establish his kingdom. He will build a house for my name, and I will establish his throne forever. I will be a father to him, and he will be a son to me. When he commits iniquity, I will punish him with a rod such as men use and with blows inflicted by men; but I will not take my mercy from him, as I did with Saul, whom I put away from before you. Your house will be permanent before my face, and your throne will be stable for eternity.

In accordance with all these words and all this vision, Nathan spoke to David; and then King David went in and sat before Yahweh, and said:

My Lord, Yahweh, who am I and what is my house that you have brought me thus far? And yet this has been a small thing in your eyes, my Lord, Yahweh, and you have spoken about the house of your servant for a great while to come, and gave advantages over the rest of the men, my Lord, Yahweh! What else can David say to you? You, O Lord, Yahweh, know your servant. You make all these great things according to your words and your heart, and make your servant know it. You are great, my Lord, Yahweh! No one is like you, and there is no God besides you, according to what we have heard with our ears. Is there on earth a people like you, Israel, that God has rescued to take to him as his own people; God gave him the name he has, and did great and awesome things for him, like rescuing him from Egypt and driving out people before you? You established your people Israel for yourself to be your people forever and you became their God. Keep forever, my Lord, Yahweh, the words you have spoken to your servant and your house, do as you have promised, and be your name magnified forever, and everybody says: Yahweh Sebaot is the God of Israel. The house of your servant David will be firm, because yourself, Yahweh Sebaot, God of Israel, has revealed yourself to your servant and said: I will build a house for you. Therefore your servant has dared to pray this prayer to you: O Lord, Yahweh! You are God, and your words are true, and you have promised to your servant this good thing. Therefore may it please you to bless the house of your servant, so that it may continue forever before you; for you, my Lord, Yahweh, have spoken, and with your blessing shall the house of your servant be blessed forever. [Here ends chapter 7 of this biblical book.]

Note that God never mentions the words "altar, temple, sanctuary, monument," or any other word referring to a material, physical structure. God used the words "build a house for you," which means "I will establish your kingdom forever." David said, "the house of your servant David," admitting that God was not talking about building a temple but about the "house of David," which means the Davidian dynasty. In other books of the Bible, the word "house" also refers to a kingdom. For instance, 1 Kings 2:24 narrates what Solomon said on the day of his coronation and before building the temple, concerning Adonijah: "Now therefore as Yahweh lives, who has confirmed me and established me in the throne of David, my father, and has made me a house, according to his promise, that Adonijah will die today."

We see in this verse that God's promise of building a "house" means to make a kingdom; Solomon admitted in this verse that before he built the temple of Jerusalem (Solomon's temple), God had already fulfilled his promise of "building a house." (Note also that from the first day of his reign, Solomon was a criminal.) In 1 Kings 11:38, the prophet Ahijah said to Jeroboam: "I will be with you, and WILL BUILD YOU AN ENDURING HOUSE, AS I BUILT FOR DAVID, AND I WILL GIVE ISRAEL TO YOU"; David didn't build the temple; it was Solomon who built the temple. Therefore we see here once more that "build a house" means to make a kingdom.

❖   ❖   ❖

Another important detail, which refers to some of the builders of the temple, indicates that the Temple of Solomon was not a holy temple. Many of the builders were Phoenicians. The Phoenicians were famous pagans who followed the religion of their neighbors, especially the Egyptian religion. In the Bible they are described as worshipers of idols. In history books we see that Phoenicians made human sacrifices. The Phoenicians and Egyptians brought the religion of pyramids, the serpent, and human sacrifices to America. Second Samuel 5:11 for the first time mentions the alliance between David and the Phoenician King Hiram; "Hiram, king of Tyre, sent messengers to David, along with cedar trees, carpenters, and masons who built the House of David." This alliance produced the building of the temple (actually made by Solomon). David violated the Law when he made this alliance with the Satanist Phoenician king.

David and his prophet Nathan lied when they said that God ordered a temple of carved stone to be built. This lie is not a surprise because David was not a holy person. He was a prominent sinner.

In this section let's study first the sins of Solomon.

First Kings 3:1 says: "Solomon made a marriage alliance with the Pharaoh, king of Egypt, he took a daughter of the Pharaoh as a wife" in clear violation of the Law, which forbade covenants with pagans. Moses took the Israelites out of Egypt, Solomon made covenants with the Pharaoh. First Kings chapter 5 narrates the alliance of Solomon with the satanic Phoenicians: "Hiram, king of Tyre, sent his messengers to Solomon when he knew he was crowned as king." This satanic alliance produced the Temple of Solomon (the "Temple of Jerusalem"). The Phoenicians, who were expert shipbuilders and seafarers, helped Solomon to build ships, according to 1 Kings 9:26 and 27: "Solomon also built ships in Asiongaber, . . . and Hiram sent his servants to help with this construction, expert seafarers, together with the servants of Solomon." Stories not well confirmed say that when the Spanish "discovered" America, they found some circumcized Indians; circumcision was practiced by the Egyptians and the Israelites.

First Kings 10:22 says about Solomon: "the king had in the sea ships of Tarshish together with the ships of Hiram, and every three years the ships arrived from Tarshish." It is believed that Tarshish was a Phoenician colony in Spain. From Spain came Columbus to America very easily. The Canary Islands are near Spain. In Peru, the Canary Islands, and Egypt, mummification and pyramid-building were common practices; this practice was taken by the Phoenicians and Egyptians to the Canary Islands and from there to America. Other routes followed by the Phoenicians from the Mediterranean coast to America are also possible. In Peru there are funerary towers called *"chulpas,"* similar to those found in Sardinia and other islands of the Mediterranean Sea. There are pyramids in the Canary Islands, which were built by the Phoenicians and Egyptians. First Kings 11:1–11 say that Solomon got married to many pagan women and that he also worshiped idols. The worship of idols in pagan nations used to include human sacrifices; therefore Solomon most probably also practiced human sacrifices. The same chapter also says "his women deviated his heart toward foreign gods," "Solomon worshiped Astarte, goddess of the Sidonians, and Milcon, abomination of the Ammonites; AND SOLOMON SINNED BEFORE THE EYES OF YAHWEH," "Yahweh was angry with Solomon because he turned his heart away from Yahweh," and it also says that Solomon "broke my covenant." The reality is that King Solomon NEVER was a follower of God. Since the beginning of his reign, he was a Satanist.

✿　　✿　　✿

Now let's see the biblical verses that describe the origin of the satanic tradition of "wisdom." (In this context "wisdom" does not simply mean to have intelligence or being wise, it is a concept given by Satan to the man in power in Sumer and Egypt, which means: having the knowledge given by Satan and believing in it, like knowing good and evil, disobeying God, and killing.)

Genesis 3:1–6 and 14: "The serpent, the most astute of all the beasts made by Yahweh in the camp, said to the woman: Did God order you not to eat of any tree in the paradise? And the woman answered to the serpent: We may eat of the fruit of the trees of paradise, but about the fruit of the tree that is in the middle of paradise, God has said: You shall not eat of it, not even touch it, or you shall die. AND THE SERPENT SAID TO THE WOMAN: No, you won't die; for God knows that the day you eat of it YOUR EYES WILL BE OPENED and you will be like God, KNOWING GOOD AND EVIL. So the woman saw that the tree was good for eating, and that it was a delight to the eyes and desirable TO OBTAIN WISDOM, and she took his fruit, and ate."

Then God said to Satan: "Because you have done this, CURSED ARE YOU AMONG ALL ANIMALS AND BEASTS OF THE CAMPS." The offering of Satan to Eve contained in 3:1 through 6 is Satan's confession of faith (or Satan's oath). This is the belief of Satan concerning theology and his relation with human behavior. Today, Satanists (including the Freemasons) called the satanic confession of faith "Dualism." David, Solomon, "Saint Paul," and Muhammad believed, swore and repeated in the Bible and the Koran the satanic confession of faith. Joseph Smith also believed in it, as written in the Book of Mormons, Hellaman 14:31, Moses 6:56, and 2 Nephi 2:26. I mentioned these in the second part of the introduction of this book. Some Bible and Koran translators use either the words "to distinguish" or the word "knowing" when talking about "knowing good and evil" or "to distinguish good from evil"; "to know" and "to distinguish" are synonymous words, according to dictionaries.

It is perfectly clear that it was Satan who taught "wisdom" to the humans. Actually Satan is the first entity in the Bible who speaks and/or uses the word "wisdom," ("wisdom" in some Bibles, "wise" in other Bibles). The first "wise" practical teaching of Satan was the killing of a human being; we see this in Genesis 4:7, which says that Cain was incited by the Devil to kill his brother Abel, and for this God told Cain: "If you do well, will you not be accepted? And if you do not do well, sin is lurking at the door? Its desire is for you, but you must master it." And Cain killed Abel. The wisdom taught by God to the human says: You shall not kill. Let's continue analyzing the life of Solomon.

After being crowned as king, Solomon's first act was a crime. We see this in 1 Kings 2:13–25 in which we read that Solomon said: "Adonias will die today. Solomon sent Banayas, son of Joyada, who stabbed him, and Adonias died."

In the following verse, we see that Solomon asks wisdom of the Devil. First Kings 3:9: "Give to your servant a prudent heart to judge your people AND ABLE TO DISCERN BE-TWEEN GOOD AND EVIL." The verses 11 and 12 add that God told him: "I give you a WISE and intelligent heart." And thus everybody got trapped in this lie, everybody had believed that Solomon asked "God" for wisdom, based only on the fact that it was Solomon himself who said that the request for wisdom was made to "God." But in the Bible, the giver of wisdom (including the ability of knowing good and evil) was Satan. Therefore Solomon asked Satan for wisdom, rather than God.

Let's continue with other perversions of Solomon.

First Kings 12:4 and 14 say clearly that Solomon was a tyrant: "your father made our yoke heavy . . ." (it is talking about Solomon, father of Rehoboam), and Rehoboam answered the Israelites: "My father made your yoke heavy, but I will add to your yoke; my father disciplined you with whips, but I will discipline you with scorpions." With similar words the Bible describes the sufferings of the Israelites in Egypt, according to Exodus 1:13 and 14: "The Egyptians became ruthless in imposing tasks on the Israelites, and made their lives bitter with hard work of mortar, brick and field labor."

In Matthew 6:28 and 29, Jesus speaks negatively about Solomon when comparing a flower with him: "Look how the lilies of the field grow: they neither toil nor spin. But I says, even Solomon in all his glory was not clothed like one of these."

✿　　✿　　✿

In the next section, I am going to explain that Solomon is the beast described in the biblical book Apocalypse (also called Revelation). We know that the Apocalypse was written by John the apostle. John took images, visions, words, and groups of words from the Old and New Testaments in order to write the Apocalypse. Almost every verse of the Apocalypse has element(s) borrowed from the Old and/or the New Testaments. Therefore a verse(s) of the Apocalypse that has no apparent meaning should be analyzed looking for similar words or ideas in the rest of the Bible. Some persons called "Midrash," the technique consisting in analyzing a Bible verse comparing it with other(s) verse(s). This is also called "Concordance," which means the relation (concordance) between one verse and other(s). For example: Apocalypse 2-7 says: "those who have ears, listen"; this verse is inspired on Matthew 13:9 and 43, which says: "those who have ears, listen." Apocalypse 2:8 says: "the first and the last"; this is based on Isaiah 44:6, which says: "I am the first and I am the last." Apocalypse 2:12 says: "the sharp two-edged sword," is based on Psalm 149:6 (not a Psalm of David), which says: "two edged-sword."

✻   ✻   ✻

Now I am going to analyze the verses of the Apocalypse that contain the clue to identify the beast 666:

Apocalypse 13:16, 17, and 18: "Also it made all, small and great, rich and poor, freed and slave, to be marked on the right hand and the forehead, and no one could buy or sell except those who had the mark, the name of the beast or the number of his name. HERE IS THE WISDOM. THE ONE WHO IS INTELLIGENT CAN GUESS THE NUMBER OF THE BEAST, BECAUSE IT IS THE NUMBER OF A MAN. HIS NUMBER IS SIX HUNDRED SIXTY-SIX."

These are the key elements of the verses to decipher the puzzle:

"small and great"
business and businessmen
"here is the wisdom"
he is a "man."
"666"

The number 666 appears in the Bible in four verses. In this one (Apocalypse 13:18) and also in one verse of the Old Testament, which is followed by another verse that has more keys to resolve the puzzle. The verses are:

1 Kings 10:14 and 15, which say: "The weight of gold that came to Solomon every year was six hundred sixty-six talents of gold, besides that which came as tribute from small and great traders, from the princes of Arabia and the governors of the land".

The key elements here are:

"Solomon"
"666"
"small and great"
business and businessmen

The concordance between these five verses are:

Apocalypse 13:16, 17 and 18	1 Kings 10:14 and 15
"small and great"	"small and great"
business and businessmen	business and businessmen
"here is the wisdom"	in "Solomon" (who represents the wisdom)
is a "man"	"Solomon"
"666"	"666"

Solomon is the beast "666." It is not a coincidence that the Satanists, among them the Freemasons, love Solomon and his temple. As I said before, the number 666 appears in the Bible only in four verses. John wrote the Apocalypse, taking ideas from the Old and New Testament. The third verse that mentions the number 666 is 2 Chronicles 9:13, which is a repetition of 1 Kings 10:14 and 15. The fourth verse that mentions the number 666 is Ezra 2:13, which says: "The sons of Adonikam, six hundred sixty and six," who are 666 who returned to Jerusalem and Judah from Babylon after the captivity. The use of this verse to analyze the number 666 concerning the concordance between Apocalypse 13:18 and 1 Kings 10:14 and 15 is nihil (non useful). I say this because the same narration in Ezra can be read in Nehemiah 7:18, which says "the son of Adonikam, six hundred sixty and SEVEN," which triggers this question: which verse is the original and correct, Ezra 2:13 (which says 666) or Nehemiah 7:18 (which says 667). Even in the case that they both say 666, they don't change the concordance between Apocalypse 13:18 and the verse that John uses to identify the beast 666:1 Kings 10:14 and 15.

Apocalypse 13:11 says: "I saw another beast that rose out of the earth and had two horns"; this is the introduction to the description of the beast 666. This verse is related to Daniel 8:20, which says: "As for the ram that you saw with the two horns, these are the kings of Media and Persia." Apocalypse 17:12 says: "The ten horns you see are ten kings." Therefore "horns" represent "kings," and therefore the beast 666 is somehow associated with two kings; actually Solomon is associated with two kings: Roboam and Jeroboam, who are the two kings who divided Israel into two portions.

Apocalypse 13:13, speaking about the beast 666: "It performs great signs, even making fire come down from heaven to earth before the eyes of all the men." The great signs referred to here are "the cloud that filled the house of Yahweh," when Solomon dedicated the temple; this is just a copy of the description of the cloud that appeared to the Israelites during the Exodus, the cloud that during the night was a column of fire. These can be read of in 1 Kings 8:10 and Exodus 13:21. The next verse is even more interesting; 2 Chronicles 7:1 says that at the dedication of the temple "when Solomon finished the prayer, fire came down from heaven." Therefore the theophanies (divine manifestations) of Apocalypse 13:13 ("signs" and "fire") refer to those in those three verses already mentioned and associated with Solomon.

Apocalypse 13:16 says: "to be marked on the right hand and the forehead." This indicates that the beast is an Israelite because this mark is inspired in Deuteronomy 6:8, which gives the commandment "Bind them on your hand as a sign, fix them on your forehead as an emblem." These theophanies narrated in the books of Kings and Chronicles are lies proceeding from Solomon, his prophet Nathan (the prophet of David and Solomon), and other liars. For these lies, John called Nathan a "false prophet." Apocalypse 16:13 says: "And I saw that from the mouth of the dragon, and from the mouth of the beast, and from the mouth of the false prophet, three filthy spirits like frogs came out; they are the spirits of the demons, those who make signs." Apocalypse 19:20 says: "And the beast was captured, and with it the false prophet who had performed signs in his presence." Apocalypse 20:9 and 10 say: "And fire came down from heaven. . . . And the devil who had deceived was thrown into the lake of fire and sulfur, where the beast and the false prophet were." Only in these three verses, the Apocalypse speaks about the false prophet. Note that he is always mentioned together with the beast in order to make clear that the false prophet is a person associated with the beast.

I have already mentioned the lies of Nathan concerning the building of the temple. Another great lie of Nathan is in 2 Samuel 12:13, which says: "David said to Nathan: I have sinned against Yahweh. And Nathan said to David: YAHWEH HAS FORGIVEN YOUR SIN"; they are talking about the killing of Uriah by David in order to get Uriah's wife. It was a lie of Nathan because David himself admitted that God didn't forgive him, according to 1 Chronicles 22:7 and 8 in which David said to Solomon: "My son, I had the purpose of building a temple to the name of Yahweh, my God, but Yahweh told me: YOU HAVE SHED MUCH BLOOD AND HAVE WAGED GREAT WARS; YOU SHALL NOT BUILD A HOUSE TO MY NAME," I already have proved that to "build a house to

God" means "to make a forever lasting Kingdom," and God rejected David for this purpose. Therefore it is nonsense to say that David was a holy man from whom the Messiah will come. Nathan (the false prophet) made a secret agreement with Betsabe (the ex-wife of Uriah who was later another wife of David and the mother of Solomon) in order to convince David to appoint Solomon as his successor; David was thinking to appoint another son as king but was finally convinced by Nathan and Betsabe to appoint Solomon, and he did so. All this can be read in 1 Kings 1:11 to 36.

The false prophet Nathan wrote his lies in the "chronicles of Nathan, prophet," in which he speaks his lies concerning David, and also in "the books of Nathan, prophet" in which he speaks the lies concerning Solomon. This is written in 1 Chronicles 29:29 and 2 Chronicles 9:29.

14. David, the First Beast of the Apocalypse

David and the false prophet Nathan were the creators of the lies concerning the holiness of the Temple of Jerusalem. Millions of people believe that David was a holy man, they believe so because they don't read the Bible. The reality is otherwise and different.

Here is a summary of David's perversion (according to the Bible):

First Samuel 19:13 says that David worshiped idols: here, Micol, one of the wives of David, "took the terafims and put them in the bed, put a skin of goat on the place of the head and cover the terafims with clothes"; this woman did that on her house (the house of David) to avoid the messengers of Saul (David's enemy) think that David was in bed while in reality David was escaping through a window. The terafims were small statues-idols of family use.

Second Samuel chapters 11 and 12 talk about how David coldly planned the killing of Uriah with the objective of taking his wife. It was a violation of the commandment that says, "You shall not kill." Second Samuel 11:27 says concerning the killing of Uriah "what David did was disagreeable before the eye of God." Uriah's wife later become a wife of David and the mother of Solomon, to which we can say that Solomon is the son of a sin, the son of a crime. If it was true that David repented for the killing of Uriah, he would not have kept Uriah's wife. Second Samuel 5:11 says, as I said before, that there was an alliance between David and the Phoenicians, which was a violation of the Law of Moses, which requires: "Do not make alliance with the inhabitants of the land to which you are going, because that will be the ruin for you. Do not make a pact with the inhabitants of those lands, for they prostitute themselves when they service their gods, and someone among them will invite you, and you will eat of the sacrifice." This can be read in Exodus 34:12, 15, and 16. Deuteronomy 7:2 says: "Make no covenant with them and show them no mercy" ("them" refers to the pagan nations).

1 Chronicles (*Paralipomenos,* in Spanish) 28:19 describes what David said about the preparation for making the temple: "All these things, he said, have been shown to me by the hands of Yahweh who gave me the design of the project," which is a lie because as I already stated, God never told David to build the temple.

Modern sciences like archaeology have shown that the Temple of Solomon practically has the same design of many ancient pagan temples. God forbade the Israelites to imitate the pagans; therefore it is a lie of David to say that God showed him the design for this temple. Besides, as I mentioned in a previous chapter, God forbade the Israelites to make temples of carved stone; and the Temple of Solomon was made of carved stone.

First Samuel 21:1–7 states that David profaned the holy tabernacle, which was the repository of the holy ark, which was the divine and untouchable jewel of the Israelites; David went in and ate of the sacred bread that, according to the Law, was reserved for the priests. David was not a king yet. First Samuel 22:2 describes David as the leader of what we would call today an antisocial gang: "Everyone who was persecuted, everyone who was in debt, and everyone who was discontented gathered to him, so he was the captain of about 400 men." First Samuel chapter 27 says that David once more made a covenant with pagans in violation of the Law of Moses; the verse says that

David joined the Philistines, the famous enemy of the Israelites; the verse 27:12 says about David: "He has made himself abhorrent to his people Israel." First Kings 2:1–9 says that "When David's time to die was near," he gave some orders to Solomon, among them to kill Joab (the general of the army who was the right hand of David for many years) and to punish Semei, an Israelite who had verbally offended David, but David had forgiven him.

Therefore David was a vengeful criminal and a person without mercy to a person who he already had forgiven; we can also see that even at the time of his death, David continued being a sinner, which invalidates the idea propagated by the prophet Nathan that God forgave David for his sins. He died as a sinner. Nathan was the prophet of David and Solomon. First Chronicles 21:1 speaks about the covenant of David with Satan: "Satan stood up against Israel and incited David to count the people of Israel," and David OBEYED him and made the census of the people of Israel (another book of the Bible says that it was God who ordered David to make the census; a secret war among the biblical writers!). DAVID PARTICIPATED IN THE PLANNING OF A HUMAN SACRIFICE according to 2 Samuel 21:1–10, which narrated that men from Gibeah asked David for seven men, for sacrificing them in Gibeah in front of "God" ("we will hang them in front of Yahweh in Gibeah").

David answered, "I will give them to you," which he did, and the sacrifice was carried out "in the first days of harvest, at the beginning of the barley harvest." The sacrifice of human beings at the beginning and the end of the harvest was a typical worldwide pagan practice. It was in this place (Gibeah, "Gibeon" in other Bibles) that Solomon used to sacrifice, and also it was there where Solomon asked for wisdom and the knowledge to distinguish between good and evil, the same place where his father David participated in a human sacrifice; therefore we now know that the petition of Solomon to "God" was in reality made to Satan in a pagan "high place" (this can be read in 1 Kings 3:1–13).

Kind David is depicted in other biblical verses as a faithful follower of God who always was on the road to God. The "false prophets" (such as Nathan) succeeded in introducing their followers and their satanism among the leadership of the so far holy Israelite religious establishment. And they cheated and confused many men of God who wrote positively about David under the belief that God forgave David of his sins, as the false prophet Nathan said. It is also possible that some of those false prophets added and eliminated biblical verses if they were convenient or not to their interests, respectively. These confusions and cheatings have been responsible for many and great disturbances, war and deaths throughout the world and since the time of David to the twentieth century. One of these deaths was the terrible murdering of Jesus Christ; his killing was the product of the lies and hypocrisy of the leaders of the Judaists, who were waiting for a Messiah descendant of the satanic David, and they cheated the innocent and ignorant crowd or mob, inciting them to cry "crucify him." The followers of the "wisdom" brought by Satan according to Genesis 3:1–6 (among them the non plus ultra of the representative of the satanic "wisdom," Solomon) spoiled the glorious and healthy road of the people of Israel.

This road started when God chose Abraham, and it continued with Moses, Elias, Isaiah, etc., which was a road that in the future should have to be strengthened with the arrival to earth of the true Messiah, Jesus Christ, sent by God to make straight the twisted road followed by the humans with the building of temples, pyramids, and with human sacrifices, ritual cannibalism, and other perversions. Those "wise" Satanists and false prophets (still active in modern times) deviated the words of God, and in doing so, they weakened the religious movement of those superheroes who were followers of God. For all these reasons (the lies, confusion, and cheating of the Satanists with holy masks), the World is today in the middle of a terrible dilemma: between life and death, between peace and war, and between the atomic holocaust, which can turn the planet into a desert inferno, and peace forever. By their satanism and because they deviated the Word of God, Solomon and David were called by John satanic "beasts."

Jesus Christ denied himself to be the descendant of David. In Matthew 22:41–45, Jesus implied that he didn't like to be called "son of David": "While the Pharisees were gathered together, Jesus asked them: What do you think of the Messiah? Whose son is he? They said to him: The son of David. He said to them: How is it then that David, moved by the Spirit, calls him Lord when he says: The Lord said to my Lord: Sit at my right hand, until I put your enemies under your feet? If David thus calls him Lord, HOW CAN HE BE HIS SON?" In Mark 12:35, Jesus asks, "HOW CAN THE SCRIBES SAY THAT THE MESSIAH IS THE SON OF DAVID?"

David was the person who initiated in the Bible the satanic wisdom tradition after Satan taught mankind this doctrine. We can see this in the following verse. Second Samuel 14:17 and 20 narrate that a woman said to King David, "Your servant thought: The word of my lord the king will set me at rest, FOR MY LORD THE KING IS LIKE AN ANGEL OF GOD, DISCERNING GOOD AND EVIL," and continues, "BUT MY LORD HAS WISDOM LIKE THE WISDOM OF THE ANGEL OF GOD to know all things that are in the earth." This is the satanic confession of faith of David. It did not come from his own mouth, but it is a description of what he is. The only angel who came to earth to teach wisdom and to distinguish between good and evil was Satan.

❈ ❈ ❈

David, the Israelite king, is the other beast described by John in the Apocalypse. David, Solomon, and Nathan (the false prophet) were responsible for all the cheating and confusion generated among the Israelites of yesterday and today. Apocalypse 13:1–10 describes the first beast in this way:

"I saw a beast rising out of the sea, it had ten horns and seven heads, and on its horns were ten diadems, and on its heads were blasphemous names. The beast that I saw was like a leopard, its feet were like a bear's, and its mouth was like the mouth of a lion. The dragon gave him his power, his throne, and great authority. I saw the first head with a mortal wound, but his mortal wound was healed. All the earth admired the beast. They adored the dragon because he had given the power to the beast, and they adored the beast, saying: Who is like the beast? Who can fight against it? The beast was given a mouth, uttering arrogance and blasphemy, and it was given authority for forty-two months. It opened its mouth to utter blasphemies against God, blaspheming his name and his tabernacle, and those who dwell in heaven. It was allowed to make war on the saints and to conquer them. It was given authority over every tribe and people and language and nation. All the inhabitants of the earth adored it, those whose names are not written since the beginning of the world in the Book of the Lamb that was killed. If someone has ears, let him listen. If someone is destined to the captivity, he will go to the captivity; if someone kills with a sword, with a sword will he be killed. In this is the patience and faith of the saints."

The following are the verses from other biblical books used by John in order to get ideas or words to describe this beast. All the following verses are somehow related to David.

Apocalypse 13:1: "Heads, and over the horns ten diadems" is based on 2 Samuel 12:30: David "Took the crown of Milcon from his head. . . . It had a precious stone, and was put on the head of David."

Apocalypse 13:2: "And his feet were like bears, and his mouth like the mouth of a lion," based on 1 Samuel 17:36: David said to Saul: "Your servant has killed lions and bears."

Apocalypse 13:3: "Everybody admired the beast," based on 1 Samuel 18:5: speaking about David it says "everybody was happy with him."

Apocalypse 13:5: "it was given authority for 42 months" refers to the years that David reigned over his people (and cooperated with the Philistines) which were in total 41 years and 10 months, which is an approximation to "42," according to 1 Kings 2:11 and 1 Chronicles 29:27. Second Samuel 5:4 and 5 say: "David was 30 years old when he started to reign, he reigned 40 years. He reigned in Hebron, over Judah, seven years and six months, and 33 years in Jerusalem, over all Israel and Judah." First Samuel 27:7 says that David was 1 year and 4 months with the Philistines.

Apocalypse 13:7 says: "It was given to him to make war against the saints and conquer them," based on 2 Samuel 2:31, which says that David made war against his own people, the Israelites: "the followers of David had mortally wounded 300 men of the tribe of Benjamin."

Apocalypse 13:7 says: "It was given authority over all tribes" is based on 2 Samuel 5:1 and 2: "All the tribes of Israel came to David, to Hebron" and they told him: "Yahweh has told you . . . be the ruler of Israel."

Apocalypse 13:10 says: "If someone is destined to the captivity, he will go the captivity," based on 1 Samuel 30:3 and 5, which says: "Sons and daughters had been taken captive. . . . The two women of David had been taken captives."

Apocalypse 13:10 says: "If someone kills with a sword, by a sword he will die" refers to the killing of Uriah ordered by David, according to 2 Samuel 12:9 and 10: "you have stabbed

Uriah with a sword; you took his woman for yours, and you kill him with the sword of the son of Ammon. For this reason the sword will never depart from your house."

Apocalypse 11:13 says: "7,000 human beings died in the earthquake," based on 1 Chronicles 19:18: "David killed 7,000 men."

Apocalypse 17:11: "As for the beast that was and is not, IT IS AN EIGHTH, BUT IT BELONG TO THE SEVEN", referring to David, who was the eighth son of Isai, according to 1 Samuel 17:12: "David was the son of an Ephrathite, of Bethlehem in Judah, who had eight sons"; 1 Samuel 16:11 says that David was the youngest, therefore the number eight: "There remains yet the youngest, but he is keeping the sheep."

These concordances indicate that John was thinking of David and talking about him, using this labyrinth of words and ideas.

15. The Satanism of Paul

The life of "Saint" Paul (Saul) is narrated in the Bible by himself and by Luke, and by some verses contained in the letters of some apostles. Paul was born in Tarsus, a city in Cilicia, in Asia Minor; he was a Jew, of the sect of the Pharisees, the sect more active against Jesus Christ. To know about the different Jewish sects, we need to read the book of Flavius Josephus. He was a Jewish historian and army commander during the war of the Jews against Rome in the first century A.D. He was also a member of the priesthood. So he was a very well informed person. After being defeated by the Romans in Jerusalem, he became allied to them. Josephus wrote two important books: *Antiquities of the Jews* and *War of the Jews.* He said that the Jews were divided into three sects: the Pharisees, the Sadducees, and the Essenes; a fourth sect similar to the Pharisees but more inclined to politics appeared during the time of the Maccabees. This can be read in *Antiquities of the Jews,* book 13 chapter 5, and book 18 chapter 1, and also in *War of the Jews,* book 2 chapter 7. The sect of the Pharisees was the largest one, very fanatic of the observance of the "Jewish tradition" but not of the Law and the teaching of the Prophets. It was a sect strongly attached to the "Davidian tradition," which included the belief that the Messiah would be a descendant of David (a terrible idea still sustained today).

Paul lived in Jerusalem where he was a fervent persecutor of the Christians, according to his own words. From Jerusalem he made expeditions to other lands to persecute Christians. In

Jerusalem, he was a disciple of the leaders of the Judaism (the religion of those who believe in God, Abraham, Moses, David and others, but they don't believe in Jesus Christ; they kill him). Gamaliel was one of those leaders who taught Paul the doctrine of Judaism. It was in Jerusalem where the Christian Stephen was killed by a Jewish mob commanded by Paul. To illustrate all these data about the life of Paul, let's review many verses of the Bible.

Acts 9:11, 21:39, and 22:3 say that there is "a man of Tarsus name Saul," who on one occasion "replied: I am a Jew, from Tarsus in Cilicia, a citizen of an important city" and in another opportunity he said "I am a Jew, born in Tarsus in Cilicia, educated in this city, instructed at the feet of Gamaliel, educated strictly according to the ancestral Law, being zealous for God." The city is Jerusalem. Acts 26:4 says, "I have lived since the beginning of my youth in Jerusalem, in the middle of my people." Acts 26:5: "I lived as Pharisee." In Romans 11:1 (a letter from Paul to his followers in Rome) Paul says that he is of the tribe of "Benjamin," one of the twelve tribes of Israel: "I am an Israelite, a descendant of Abraham, of the tribe of Benjamin." And about his teacher Gamaliel, Acts 5:34 says that during a debate about Paul: "a Pharisee in the council named Gamaliel, a teacher of the Law, respected by all the people, stood up and ordered the men to be put outside for a short time."

The Book of Acts was supposedly written by Luke a collaborator of Paul. Acts 7:54–60 says that they took Stephen "out of the city and began to stone him. The witnesses laid their coats at the feet of a young man named Saul . . . and Stephen died. And Saul approved of their killing him"; Saul there shows that he is a murderer. Acts 8:3 says that "Saul was ravaging the church by entering house after house dragging off both men and women and taking them to prison."

Acts 9:1 and 2 says: "Saul, still breathing threats of murder against the disciples of the Lord, went to the high priest and asked him for a letter of recommendation to the synagogues at Damascus, so that if he found anyone who were Christians, men or women, he might bring them bound to Jerusalem." Acts 9:14 says, "he has authority from the chief priest to bind all who invoke your name." Acts 9:21 says of Paul: "Is this not the man who persecuted in Jerusalem those who invoke the name of the Lord? And has he not come here for the purpose for bringing them here bound to the chief priest?" Acts 22:4 and 5 say, "I persecuted this doctrine up to the point of death by binding men and women and putting them in prison, as the high priest and the whole counsel of elders can testify about me. From them I also received letters to the brothers in Damascus, and I went there in order to bind those who were there and to bring them to Jerusalem for punishment."

Therefore the anti-Christian work of Paul was supervised by the high authority of Judaism, the same authority that killed Jesus Christ years before. Acts 22:19: "They themselves note that in every synagogue I imprisoned and beat those who believe in the Lord." Acts 26:11: Paul says that he persecuted the Christians: "By punishing them often in all the synagogues." In his letter to the Galatians 1:11–24, Paul says that he "persecuted the Church of God and destroyed it." In 1 Corinthians 15:9, Paul admits, "I am not worthy of being called apostle, because I persecuted the Church of God." First Timothy 1:13 says, "I first was a blasphemer and a violent persecuter of the Christians." So we clearly see that Paul was an anti-Christian who obeyed orders from the high authority of the synagogues and the Temple of Jerusalem.

In one of his trips to Damascus to persecute Christians, Paul said that he saw a vision of Jesus Christ, which convinced him to become a Christian. Luke speaks about this in Acts 9:3–8: "He was near Damascus: suddenly he saw a light from the sky; and he fell to the ground and heard a voice saying to him: Saul, Saul, why do you persecute me? He asked, Who are you, Lord? The Lord said, I am Jesus, whom you are persecuting. But get up and enter the city and you will be told what you are to do. . . . Saul got up from the ground and though his eyes were open, he could see nothing." Chapter 9 verse 20 says: "He began to proclaim Jesus in the synagogues, saying that Jesus is the son of God." Acts 22:6–21 and 26:12–18 contains the supposed conversion of Paul narrated by himself. From this moment Paul started his "Christian" and missionary activities. Based on this lie about the conversion of Paul to Christianity, he could infiltrate as a Trojan horse the Christian movement.

Based on Paul's teachings, a whole body of doctrine called "Pauline" has been created. The Vatican bases many of their teachings on the Pauline doctrine. The Christians have been following the teachings of Paul and the Vatican with the subsequent results: millions of dead and tortured people, frequent persecutions and wars directed by the leaders of the Vatican. For this reason people have to understand that the Inquisition was not an organism created by God to bring peace and justice to earth, but an instrument of Satan to bring death and a chain of pain to humans. The creation of the Inquisition was not a mistake of the Vatican; it was the product of its satanism, subtly hidden behind the mask of Christianity. Because few Christians study and read the Bible, the Vatican's lies are alive today. A sequential and complete study of the Bible clearly reveals the hidden satanism of Paul.

Jesus Christ chose twelve apostles for his missionary activities. One of them, Judas, committed suicide, leaving the number as eleven. These apostles formed a compact group with their base in Jerusalem. Paul never was a member of this group. The apostles rejected Paul and Paul denigrated them. In the following verses, we see the enmity between Paul and the Apostles. We can see this enmity not only in the harsh interchange of accusations, but also in the many lies that Paul created about the Apostles.

Before this is discussed, we have to know that the Book of Acts contains many of the lies about the Apostles. It is said that this book was written by Luke, a Jewish medical doctor, and a member of the group of Paul; no verse of this book mentions the name of the author. Luke was a member of the group of Paul, according to the following verses written in letters by Paul: Letters to the Colossians 4:14: "Luke, the beloved physician, and Demas greet you," he said this at the end of the letter as a salutation. Second Timothy 4:11: "only Luke is with me"; Paul is talking here about some of his followers who abandoned him, except for Luke. In the letter of Paul to Philemon, verses 23 and 24, Paul says, "Epaphras, my fellow prisoner in Jesus Christ, and also Demas and Luke, my fellow workers"; therefore we see clearly that Luke was a collaborator with Paul. Luke speaks extensively about Paul in his book, Acts of the Apostles, and says very few words about the apostles of Christ. Luke also wrote one of the four gospels. There are data indicating: 1) Paul was the writer of the "Gospel of Luke" and the Acts of the Apostles, or 2) the opinions of Luke in these two books are a copy of Paul's teachings.

Paul had written a gospel, as he said in his Letter to the Romans, 16:25: "God who is able to strengthen you according to my gospel." Second Timothy 2:8 says: "Remember Jesus Christ, raised from the dead, a descendant of David, according to my gospel." The Gospel of Luke does not give the name of the author in any verse, but the introduction is similar to the letter of Paul: This gospel says in the introduction that it is addressed to Theophilus (Luke 1:3). It is interesting to know that Theophilus is the same to whom Luke dedicated his book Acts of the Apostles. Luke 1:3 says, "I too decided, after investigating everything carefully from the very beginning, to write an orderly account for you, most excellent Theophilus." Acts 1:1 says: "In the first book, O excellent Theophilus!, I wrote about the work and teaching of Jesus."

There are many similarities between the writings of Luke and Paul, sufficient enough to make us think that the writing has the same author. For example, Luke 22:19: "Then he took a loaf of bread, and when we had given thanks, he broke it and gave it to them saying: this is my body, which is given for you; do this in remembrance of me." This is similar to 1 Corinthians 11:23 and 24: Jesus "took a loaf of bread, and when he had given thanks, he broke it and said, this is my body that is for you, do this in remembrance of me." This similarity does not exist in the writings of the other three gospel authors, Matthew, Mark, and John. In the book Acts of the Apostles, when the author is speaking about Paul, frequently he uses the word "us" or he writes in the first person, meaning that the author is Paul himself or that Luke was present during the incidents that are written about. Also we will see that the writing of Luke has satanic concepts similar to those of Paul.

The following are verses that contain lies of Paul and Luke about the apostles, which show that they were enemies. Acts 1:6: the apostles asked Christ after the resurrection, "Lord, is this the time when you will restore the kingdom of Israel?" Here Luke accuses the apostles of being ignorant and Judaists; he accuses them of focusing on the arrival of the human Messiah, which was the expectation of the Pharisees; that means the Pharisees were waiting for the arrival of a warrior king full of wisdom who would be the master of the world. The apostles knew very well at this time of their lives (a few days before the ascension of Jesus Christ) that the expectation of the Pharisees was false and opposed to the doctrine of Jesus Christ. Acts 2:46 and 5:42 say that the apostles frequently visited the Temple of Jerusalem after the death of Christ, which is a lie because the apostles knew that Jesus Christ had broken with the Jewish practices and beliefs, including the adoration of the Temple of

Solomon, which was the seat of those who killed Jesus Christ. Acts 4:13: Here Luke accuses Peter and John of being ignorant "when they saw the freedom of Peter and John, and considered that they were uneducated and plebeians"; someone who reads the letters of Peter and John easily realizes that they were very well educated and illustrious.

Acts 5:1–11: here Luke made one of the greatest false assertions about Peter. Luke says that Peter killed a man and his wife because they were not good members of the church: "Peter told them: Ananias, Satan has filled your heart to the point of lying to the Holy Spirit, . . . you have not lied to men, but to God. When Ananias heard those words, he fell down and died." Later, Peter talked to the wife of Ananias and asked: Why have you agreed together to tempt the Holy Spirit? . . . Immediately she fell down at his feet and died." Peter knew the teachings of Jesus Christ, which said, "You shall not kill" and forgive the sinner; therefore this opinion of Luke should not be believed.

Acts 10:13–16 describes a vision that Peter had in which he saw a "big tablecloth," filled with animals and birds, and Peter heard a voice saying "kill and eat," and Peter answered, "I never have eaten something impure." Here Luke accuses Peter of not eating of certain foods for religious reasons, which really was a Jewish practice. Jesus Christ rejected the practices of the Judaists, including not to eat pork; Peter learned this teaching of Jesus; therefore we should not believe this lie of Luke. Acts 10:28: here Luke accuses Peter of keeping the Jewish belief of not having close relations with non-believers; in this verse Luke also said that Peter finally "accepted" the teaching of the vision of the tablecloth; so Luke said that Peter changed his opinion and accepted to eat every food and to have relations with pagans.

The goal of these Luke stories is to depict Peter as a follower and keeper of the "Jewish tradition" and therefore to show that Peter was not a good Christian (actually this is the intention of Luke: to picture Peter as a bad Christian). Acts 18:22 says that Paul "went to Jerusalem and greet the church, and later went to Antioch." In 21:15 it says that Paul went to "Jerusalem." Paul is never described as member of the Jerusalem church. To the contrary, they opposed each other, and although Paul visited a few times the church (the Christians) of Jerusalem, he NEVER was associated with the apostles. Acts 21:4 refers to Paul being advised not to go to Jerusalem: "We found disciples in Tyre, . . . They, moved by the Holy Spirit, said to Paul not to go to Jerusalem," which is a subtle way of saying that Paul and the apostles were enemies and therefore that it was not convenient for Paul to go to Jerusalem. Something similar can be read in Acts 22:17–21 in which Paul said, "When I returned to Jerusalem, I fell into a trance while praying in the temple, and I saw the Lord who told me: HURRY AND GET OUT OF JERUSALEM QUICKLY, BECAUSE THEY WILL NOT ACCEPT YOUR TESTIMONY ABOUT ME. . . . Go, for I will send you far away to the Gentiles"; also notice that Paul prays on the Temple of Jerusalem (a temple rejected by the apostles who never went back to that temple after the death of Christ).

Galatians 1:17 and 18 say about Paul: "I didn't go to Jerusalem to those who were already apostles before me, but I went to Arabia and then I returned to Damascus. Then after three years I went to Jerusalem to visit Cephas (Peter), and stayed with him fifteen days." So, Paul met Peter, but didn't become a member of the group of apostles who were chosen by Christ. When Paul became a "Christian," he knew that the apostles would not believe on him; we read this in Acts 9:26: "When he arrived in Jerusalem, he wanted to joint the disciples, but they all were afraid of him, for THEY DIDN'T BELIEVE THAT HE WAS A DISCIPLE."

Other verses that show the discord and enmity between Paul and the apostles are the following.

Romans 16:17 and 18 (a letter from Paul to his followers in Rome) says: "I recommend you, brothers, to keep an eye on those who cause dissensions and scandals against the doctrine you have learned, and go away from them; they don't serve our Lord Jesus Christ, but their own appetite, and for using smooth talk and flattery they deceived the heart of the unwary."

First Corinthians 1:10–12: "I appeal to you, brothers, . . . don't have schisms among you, . . . I say this, brothers, because I have known by Cloe's people that there are discords among you and that each of you say: 'I belong to Paul', or 'I belong to Apollos,' or 'I belong to Cephas (Peter),' or 'I belong to Christ.'" Cephas is another name for Peter. The whole of chapter 3 is about this enmity.

First Corinthians 9:2–4: "If I AM NOT AN APOSTLE TO OTHERS, at least I am to you, for you are the seal of my apostleship in the Lord. And this is my defense against those who debate with me: Do we not have the right for eating and drinking? Do we not have the right to be accompanied by a wife, as do the other apostles and the brothers of the Lord and Cephas?" We see clearly that the true apostles didn't believe that Paul was an apostle.

First Corinthians 11:18: Paul says: "For, to begin with, I heard that when you come together there are schisms among you, and to some extent I believe it."

First Corinthians 15:9 and 10: Paul says: "For I am the least of the apostles, I am unworthy to be called apostle, because I persecuted the church of God . . . I worked harder than any of them"; this last means that he had worked more than the other apostles, according to him.

First Corinthians 16:8 and 9: Paul says: "I will stay in Ephesus until Pentecost, for a wide door has opened to me, although there are many adversaries."

Chapters 11 and 12 of the second letter to the Corinthians are also very clear in showing the enmity between Paul and the apostles. For example, 2 Corinthians 11:5: "I think that I am not inferior to these illustrious apostles." Second Corinthians 11:13–15: Paul says: "FOR SUCH FALSE APOSTLES, DE-CEITFUL WORKERS, THEY DISGUISE THEMSELVES AS APOSTLES OF CHRIST; AND NO WONDER! EVEN SATAN DISGUISES HIMSELF AS AN ANGEL OF LIGHT. SO IT IS NOT STRANGE THAT HIS MINISTERS DIS-GUISE THEMSELVES AS MINISTERS OF THE RIGH-TEOUSNESS; THEIR END WILL CORRESPOND WITH THEIR WORKS."

Paul dares to says blasphemous words against the apostles of Jesus Christ. The lecture of these two verses is enough to convince us that Paul was an anti-Christian. Christians believe that Paul is another Christian only and exclusively because no one reads the Bible orderly, judiciously, objectively, and care-fully; we are accustomed to read the Bible by jumping from two to three verses of one chapter to two or three more verses of other chapters (usually of other books). When reading the Bible in this way, we cannot see the connection and concor-dance between one verse and other(s) verse in the same book or other book. To understand the Bible, we have to read it sequentially, verse by verse, from the first one in Genesis to the last one in the Apocalypse.

Second Corinthians 12:11: Paul says: "I have been a fool!; you forced me to it . . . for I am not inferior to these illustrious apostles, even though I am nothing."

Galatians 1:6–8 (a letter of Paul to his followers in Galatia): "I am astonished that you are so quickly abandoning the one who called you in the grace of Christ, AND ARE TURNING TO A DIFFERENT GOSPEL, NOT THAT THERE IS AN-OTHER GOSPEL, BUT THERE ARE SOME WHO ARE DISTURBING YOU AND PRETENDING TO PERVERT

THE GOSPEL OF CHRIST. BUT EVEN IF WE OR AN ANGEL FROM HEAVEN PROCLAIM TO YOU A GOSPEL CONTRARY TO WHAT WE PROCLAIMED TO YOU, LET THAT ONE BE ACCURSED." In this two verses, we can see that: Paul has his own gospel (probably the one now attributed to Luke), second, that many abandoned him, and third, that he doesn't even respect the angels (a terrible thing at that time).

Galatians 4:15–17: "Where is that goodwill you had to me? . . . Have I become your enemy by telling you the truth? They flatter you, and not for your good; they pretend to take you away from me in order you flatter them."

Philippians 1:15–26 (a letter of Paul to his followers in Philippi): says among other things "There are some who proclaim Christ out of envy and rivalry."

Colossians 2:18: "Don't allow anyone with the cult of the angels to disqualify you, making ostentation of what they have seen. . . ." Paul refers to the apostles who had seen Jesus Christ.

Second Timothy 1:15: Paul says, "You know how many in Asia have turned away from me, including Phygelus and Hermogenes"; this indicates that frequently his followers abandoned him. Chapter 4, verses 10 and 11 say, "Demas has abandoned me . . . only Luke is with me." Verse 16 says, "In my first defense no one helped me, they all abandoned me."

Another topic frequently mentioned by Paul is that of circumcision. Paul accused the apostles of keeping the Jewish tradition of circumcision. As I said before, Jesus broke with the Jewish tradition; therefore we should not believe that the apostles still believed in circumcision. In neither the letters of the Apostles nor in the Gospels of Matthew, Mark, and John do we find proof that the apostles believed in circumcision; these accusations are only written by Luke and Paul. For example: In Acts 10:44 and 45, Luke says, "While Peter was still speaking, the holy spirit fell upon all who heard the word; the believers of circumcision who came with Peter were astounded that the holy spirit had been poured out even to the Gentiles"; in this verse Luke also accused Peter of keeping the Jewish tradition of nonassociation with Gentiles.

Acts 11:1–3 says: "The apostles and the brothers of Judah heard that even the Gentiles had received the word of God. But when Peter went to Jerusalem, he disputed with those who believed in circumcision, saying: You have been with the noncircumcised and have eaten with them." Acts 15:1–4: "Some that came from Jerusalem were teaching the brothers: If you do not circumcise according to the Law of Moses, you will not be saved. Because of this there was a great disturbance and a dispute, and Paul and Barnabas were against them." These two last people "upon arrival to Jerusalem were welcomed by the church and the apostles," which is an obvious lie. Actually it was Paul who believed in circumcision, according to Acts 16:1–3, which says: "Paul went to Derbe and Lystra where there was a disciple named Timothy, the son of a Jewish woman who was a believer and his father was a Greek, Timothy was very well recommended by the brothers of Listra and Iconium. Paul wanted Timothy to accompany him, and he took him and had him circumcised because of the Jewish who were in those places."

It is part of the style of Paul to write in a confusing and contradictory manner, he did so deliberately with the purpose of hiding his satanism. For example, in Romans 2:25, Paul says, "Circumcision is indeed of value if you obey the Law; but if you break the Law, your circumcision becomes foreskin." Romans 3:1 says: "Then, what advantage has the Jew? Or what is the value of circumcision? Much, in every way." We see here that Paul is the one who defends circumcision. Romans 3:30 says: "There is only one God, that justifies circumcision by the faith and the foreskin by the faith"; (the word "foreskin" is the literal translation of the Spanish word *prepucio*, in this context "foreskin" probably means uncircumcision).

94

Romans 15:8 also speaks another lie and blasphemy of Paul: "For I tell you that Christ was a minister of the circumcision on behalf of the truth of God, to fulfill the promises of the fathers." First Corinthians 7:19: "Circumcision is nothing, the foreskin is nothing, if you do not keep the precepts of God." In Galatians 2:4–14, Paul criticizes the "false brothers," saying "on the contrary, when they saw that I received the gospel of the uncircumcision, as Peter received the gospel of the circumcision (for he who worked through Peter, making him an apostle of the circumcision, also worked through me in sending me to the Gentiles), and when James and Cephas (Peter) and John, considered to be the pillars, recognized the grace that had been given to me, they gave to Barnabas and me the hand as a sign of communion, agreeing that we should go to the gentiles and they to the circumcised"; other Bibles says the "right hand," which implies a concept related to the posture of the Pharaoh, sacrificing enemies. And "when CEPHAS CAME TO ANTIOCH, I OPPOSED HIM TO HIS FACE, BECAUSE HE STOOD SELF-CONDEMNED. . . . BUT WHEN I SAW THAT THEY WERE NOT ACTING CONSISTENTLY WITH THE TRUTH OF THE GOSPEL, I SAID TO CEPHAS BEFORE THEM ALL: If you, though a Jew, live like a gentile and not like a Jew, how can you compel the Gentiles to live like Jews?"

It was Paul who defended the Jewish tradition as we can read in 1 Corinthians 11:2: "I commend you because you remember me and maintain the traditions that I have transmitted to you." Galatians 6:12 and 13 says: "It is those who want to make a good showing in the flesh that try to compel you to be circumcised and not to be persecuted by the cross of Christ. Even the circumcised do not keep the Law, but they want you to be circumcised so that they may boast about your flesh." Philippians 3:2 says: "Beware of the dogs, beware of the evil-workers, beware of mutilation; because we are the circumcision, we worship the holy spirit and boast in Christ Jesus and have no confidence in the flesh"; here Paul called the apostles of Jesus Christ "dogs." The following verses spoken by Paul also express strong and blasphemous opinions about the apostles of Jesus: Titus 1:10 and 14 says: "There are many undisciplined, idle talkers, charlatans and deceivers, especially those of the circumcision, whose mouth should be closed . . . and do not pay attention to the Jewish myth."

These were the biblical verses in which Luke and Paul showed that they were enemies of the Apostles of Jesus Christ to the point that Paul called them "ministers" of Satan.

     ❁   ❁   ❁

Let's look at other verses that show the evil mentality of Paul. Acts 13:6–12 states that Paul made a magician blind, an attitude contrary to the mercy and teachings of Jesus Christ: In Paphos "they found a magician, false prophet, Jew, named Bar-Jesus . . . but Saul, also known as Paul, filled with the holy spirit, staring at his eyes, told him: right now the hand of the Lord is against you and you will be blind for a certain time, unable to see the sun"; while Jesus Christ made the blind see, Paul blinded this man, but also this is a blasphemy for Paul to say that he made this man blind in the name of Jesus Christ. First Timothy 1:19 and 20 say that Paul gave two men to Satan, even knowing that Jesus Christ came to free humans from Satan.

Paul says: ". . . having faith and a good conscience. Some who lost them suffered shipwreck in the faith; among them Hymenaeus and Alexander, WHOM I HAVE TURNED OVER TO SATAN, so that they may learn not to blaspheme." Acts 18:18: "Paul, . . . after he shaved his hair at Cenchreae because he was under a vow . . ."; this shaving is a violation of the Law of Moses, according to Leviticus 21:1, 5, and 10, and 19:27, which say: "Yahweh told Moses: speak to the priests who are sons of Aaron and tell them: . . . do not shave your head," and "do not shave all around your head" because this is a pagan practice done by the Egyptian priests. Acts 21:26 says that Paul continued being a Judaist even after his "conversion to Christianity" by attending the Temple of Jerusalem: "Paul took several men and the next day, having purified himself, he entered the temple, making public the completion of the days. . . ."

First Timothy 4:8 also reveals the Judaism of Paul: he advised his followers not to participate in physical training "because the physical gymnastics is of poor benefit." Paul took this idea from 2 Maccabees 4:9, 12, and 13, which criticizes these customs of physical training. Acts 23:6 and 9: after his "conversion" to Christianity, Paul was accused by some Jews of causing dissension and he was taken before the council. Then "Paul knew that some were Sadducees and others were Pharisees, he shouted at the Sanhedrin: Brothers, I am a Pharisee and a son of Pharisees . . . and in the middle of a great dissension some doctor of the sect of the Pharisees rose up and violently disputed, saying: We find nothing wrong with this man;" meaning that Paul was not guilty of causing dissension. The reason the Pharisees defended Paul is that they knew Paul was really a Pharisee and not a Christian, as Paul himself used to say; the supposed conversion of Paul happened between A.D. 34 and 36 and this declaration of being a Pharisee happened around the year A.D. 57.

Romans 1:16 and 2:10 also expresses that Paul is a follower of Judaism and not Christianity: "but glory and honor and peace for everyone who does good, the Jewish first and then for the Gentile." The malice and cynicism of Paul are shown, as I already mentioned in his writing style, which is confusing and contradictory to the point that he admits himself in several verses that he writes that way deliberately. For example, Romans 2:10 after saying, "the Jewish first," in the next verse, he adds "for God shows no partiality"; and in Romans 10:12, he says, "There is no distinction between Jewish and Gentile." In 1 Corinthians 15:14 and 15, there is another confusing game of words: "And if Christ has not been raised, then our proclamation has been in vain and your faith has been in vain. We are even found to be misrepresenting God, because we testified of God THAT HE RAISED CHRIST, WHOM HE DID NOT RAISE, BECAUSE THE DEAD DO NOT RESUSCITATE." In 1 Corinthians 15:34, Paul says, "I say this to confuse you," so Paul is aware of his own confusing style. For this reason Jude called him in verse 18 of his book, "buffoon." In 2 Corinthians 10:9 and 10, Paul says, "I do not want to seem as though I am trying to frighten you with my letters. For they say: His letters are weighty and strong, but his bodily presence is weak, and his speech contemptible." Second Corinthians 12:16: "Nevertheless, since I was crafty, I took you in by deceit."

❖ ❖ ❖

The following verses also contain harsh blasphemies of Paul.

Romans 4:15: "the Law brought wrath. . . ." Romans 5:20: "The Law was introduced to make more abundant the sin." Deliberately he contradicts himself in 1 Timothy 1:8 "We know that the Law is good." Paul says against the Law, "We know the person is justified not by the works of the Law but through faith in Jesus Christ!" (Galatians 2:15 and 16).

Other verses of Paul against the Law are in Romans 3:20, 27, and 28, and 4:14, also in 1 Corinthians 9:20, and Philippians 3:9. In Romans 15:8, Paul says, "I say to you that Christ was a minister of circumcision." First Corinthians 11:14 states, "Does not nature itself teach you that if a man wears long hair, it is degrading to him?" He is talking about Christ, who wore long hair. In Ephesians 2:15, Paul says about Christ, "He has abolished the Law with its commandments and ordinances," which

98

is a lie because Christ said that he came to make the Law more perfect. Colossians 2:10: Paul says about Christ, "And you are full of Him, HE IS THE HEAD OF ALL RULERS AND AUTHORITIES." These rulers and authorities are demons, according to Paul in his letter to the Ephesians 6:12, in which he says, "For our struggle is not against enemies of blood and flesh, but AGAINST THE RULERS, AGAINST THE AUTHORITIES, against the cosmic powers of this present darkness, against the spiritual darkness of evil in the heavenly places."

In Galatians 3:13, Paul says, "Christ redeemed us from the CURSE OF THE LAW BY BECOMING A CURSE FOR US, FOR IT IS WRITTEN: CURSED IS EVERYONE WHO HANGS ON A TREE." Clearly Paul is cursing Jesus Christ, because he mentions Christ and the hanging within the same sentence that clearly refers to Jesus Christ hanging on the cross; the blasphemy is obvious. In Colossians 2:3, Paul accuses Christ of being a follower of the Satanic tradition of "wisdom." "And know the mystery of God, this means, Jesus Christ, in whom are hidden all the treasures of wisdom and science"; this "science" is the "science of the tree of good and evil," from which Satan offered his fruit to the human so they could learn "wisdom" (read Genesis 2:9 and 3:6). Hebrews 6:1 (a letter of Paul to his followers the Hebrews) says: "Therefore let us put aside the elementary doctrine about Christ, and let us go toward perfection"; we will see later that perfection means learning to distinguish between good and evil.

An important topic in the theology of Paul is the false belief that salvation comes only through faith. According to Paul, it does not matter if we are good fathers or mothers, or bad neighbors, or bad sons or daughters; nothing can condemn us; we are only condemned if we lack faith. This fanatical and false idea of Paul is written in many verses. For example, in Romans 1:17, Paul says, "The one who is righteous will live by faith." Romans 3:28 says, "For we hold that a person is justified by faith apart from works prescribed by the Law." Romans 4:16 says, "For this reason the promise comes by faith." Galatians 2:16 says, "A person is justified not by the works of the Law, but through faith in Jesus Christ." Other verses speaking in the same tenor are Ephesians 2:8 and 9: Philippians 3:9, and others.

In a previous chapter, I clearly proved that David was a Satanist. Paul is a defender of David, according to the following verses: Romans 1:3 says, "The gospel concerning his Son, who was descended from David according to the flesh." Second Timothy 2:8 says, "Remember Jesus Christ, raised from the dead, a descendant of David, that is my gospel, ..." In Acts 13:22, 23, and 36, Luke says that Paul expressed the following, "When we had removed him, he made David their king, of whom he gave testimony, saying, I have found David, son of Jesse, to be a man after my heart, and he will do everything according to my will. Of this man's posterity God has brought to Israel a savior Jesus as he promised." Verse 36 says, "For David, after he had served during his life the will of God, he died and was laid beside his ancestors."

This verse explains the reason why Paul simulated a conversion to Christianity and joined the Christian movement as a leader: Christ cut the umbilical cord, which connected the Jews and the world, from the satanic David and his followers (including the Pharisees); Paul was commanded to connect again David and his ideas with the followers of God, and once again the holy movement of the followers of God was perverted. The perversion still persists today to the point that the Christian believes in the doctrine of Paul. By believing in the theology of Paul during 1974 years, the world has only seen death, rebellions, and wars; millions of humans have died defending David and Paul (and the Vatican) under the belief that they are defending Judaism and/or Christianity; these millions died ignorant of their deceit.

Although it is not necessarily related to Satanism, let's read the opinion of Paul about women; Paul denigrated women, as Muhammad did five centuries later. Compare their opinions with the opinion of Christ toward women. In 1 Corinthians 7:10 and 13, Paul says, "to the married I give this command, it is not my precept, but God's precept that the wife should not separate from her husband . . . and if any woman has a husband who is an adulterer and he consents to live with her, she should not divorce him."

First Corinthians 11:3 and 10 says, "But I want you to understand that Christ is the head of every man, and the husband is the head of his wife; and for this reason a woman should have a sign of authority on her head out of respect for the angels." First Corinthians 14:34 says, "Women should be silent in the churches, for they are not permitted to speak, but should be subordinated, as the Law says." Paul says here that the Law is good, contrary to other verses in which he said that the Law only brought sins. Jesus Christ clarified that Moses gave strong laws to the Israelites because they had hard hearts. Ephesians 5:22–24 says, "The married women should be subject to their husbands as men are to the Lord, for the husband is the head of the wife . . . just as the church is subject to Christ, so also wives should be in everything subject to their husbands." This is also the belief of the Vatican, which based its doctrine on Paul's teachings. Colossians 3:18 says, "The wives should be subject to their husbands as it is convenient for the Lord." First Timothy 2:11 and 12: "The women should learn in silence with full submission. I don't permit any woman to talk or to have authority over a man, instead she has to keep silence." This opinion can only originate in an abusive, evil mentality. Titus 2:5 says: the women should be "submissive to their husbands."

In the first century A.D., a new religious sect was born. They called themselves "Gnostics." This satanic religious group maintained that the soul is entrapped and suffering in the human body. They believed the human body is inclined toward degeneration. They also claimed to be in possession of an ancient knowledge that brings salvation. (*Gnosis* means knowledge.) They had a syncretic theology: they assimilated pagan and Christian ideas. Paul did the same: he connected paganism with Christianity. Paul contributed to the birth of Gnosticism, giving them ideas that they used. For example:

Romans 7:18, 24 and 25: "I know that there is nothing on me, in my flesh, anything good" and "Wretched man that I am! Who will rescue me from this body of death? Thanks be to God through Jesus Christ our Lord . . . with my mind I am a slave to the Law of God, but with my flesh I am a slave to the Law of sin." First Corinthians 9:27: "but I punish my body and enslave it." Colossians 3:5: "Put to death, therefore, whatever in you is earthly." Galatians 5:17: "The flesh has tendencies contrary to the spirit, and the spirit has tendencies contrary to the flesh; they are opposed to each other, to prevent you from doing what you want." Also based on these ideas, many Christian monks mortified and punished their bodies (sometimes using whips) sometimes to the point of bleeding in order to purify the body; this was a violation of the biblical law of not making incisions on the body.

The satanic "wisdom" tradition was deeply rooted among many Jews. Paul also believed in the wisdom offered by Satan to the humans. Many verses in the the books of Paul show his belief and obedience to the wisdom of the Serpent. Romans 11:33: "OH THE DEPTH OF THE RICHES AND WISDOM AND THE SCIENCE OF GOD! How unsearchable are his judgments and how inscrutable his ways!" Remember that Paul is talking here about the wisdom given by Satan to the humans when he made them eat of the fruit of the tree of the science of good and evil in the paradise.

First Corinthians 2:6 and 7: "We speak, among the perfects, a wisdom that does not belong to this age, or of the princes of this age, who are doomed to perish; instead we teach a divine wisdom, mysterious, hidden, predestined by God before this age for our glory"; before the age at the beginning of time, Satan taught his divine, mysterious wisdom to humans, according to Genesis. Like Solomon, Paul deceived us, saying that the wisdom came from God, but those who read the Bible carefully know the truth about this topic.

First Corinthians 12:8: "To someone it is given the word of wisdom; to others the word of science." Ephesians 1:8: "superabundantly he poured over us IN PERFECT WISDOM and prudence." Ephesians 1:17 and 18: "For the God of our Lord Jesus Christ and Father of the glory may give you a spirit of wisdom and revelation as you to come to know him, illuminating the eyes of your hearts"; here he is talking about the wisdom taught by Satan to Eve, which "opened the eye" of humans and made them see that wisdom. Ephesians 3:9 and 10: "and give them light about the dispensation of the mystery occulted since before this age in God, creator of everything, for the multiform wisdom of God should be announced by the church to the rulers and authorities in heaven." Colossians 1:28: Christ "whom we proclaim, warning everyone and teaching them in all wisdom so that we may present PERFECT to Jesus Christ." Colossians 2:2, 3 and 23: "so that they may have all the riches of the intelligence and may know the mystery of God, which is Christ, in whom are hidden all the treasures of the wisdom and the science" and "They are precepts, which implies a certain kind of wisdom." The Satanists Paul and Muhammad frequently use the words "wisdom" and "science" in the same verse; I have already given the meaning of these words.

Colossians 3:16: "Let the word of Christ dwell in you abundantly, teaching and admonishing one another with all wisdom,

103

with psalms . . ." THE TRUE APOSTLES OF GOD CRITI-
CISED THE WISDOM IN THEIR LETTERS OR DO NOT
MENTION IT AT ALL; Paul is the only one who speaks abundantly about the wisdom, making eulogy about it, which is an
expression of his satanism.

❖   ❖   ❖

Having proved the Satanism of Paul according to his belief
and work, I will continue now analyzing his own confession
of Satanic faith, which is written in a letter to his followers,
the Hebrews:

In Hebrews 5:10–13 and 6:1, Paul says, "About this we
have much to say that is hard to explain, since you have become
dull in understanding. For after so many times you should be
teachers, but you need someone to teach you again the basic
elements of the divine oracles, and now you need milk instead
of solid food. For everyone who lives on milk is not able to
understand the doctrine of justice, because he is still a child;
but the solid food is for the perfect for those who according to
their custom have the senses exercised TO DISTINGUISH
BETWEEN GOOD FROM EVIL. Therefore, let us put aside
the elementary doctrines about Jesus Christ and let us go on
toward perfection."

We see clearly here that "after so many times," meaning
since the time of Adam and Eve, which was the time when the
serpent gave the humans "basic elements of the divine oracles,"
the human forgot his doctrine, but it has not been forgotten by
those "who according to their custom" (the Jewish satanists who
love the "tradition") have "the senses exercised to distinguish
good from evil" (they have been doing this for three thousand
years). Paul is evidently talking about Genesis 3:1–6. Paul called
the followers of the doctrine of wisdom "perfect." He does the
same in 1 Corinthians 2:6: "We speak, nonetheless, among the

104

perfect, a wisdom that does not belong to this age," and Colossians 1:28: Christ "to whom we proclaim . . . instructing you in all wisdom in order to present you perfect to Jesus Christ." The similarity between these last two verses an Hebrews 5:13 (and the use of the word "perfect") proves that the letter to the Hebrews was written by Paul.

There is an old debate concerning the real author of the letter to the Hebrews, which is the only letter of Paul that does not mention the name of the author. Other similarities that prove that Paul is the author of the letter to the Hebrews are the following: The letter ends in the typical manner that Paul used to end his letters. At the end of the letter to the Hebrews, he mentions Timothy, who is a follower of Paul and he is never mentioned by the apostles. The end of the letter to the Hebrews says in 13:21–25, "Through Jesus Christ, to whom be the glory for ever and ever. Amen . . . our brother Timothy has been set free and if he comes in time, he will be with me when I see you. Greet all you pastors and all the saints . . . grace be with all of you." Paul ends all of the other letters in the same manner, as I will show you.

Romans 16:27 says, "Through Jesus Christ, to whom be the glory for ever. Amen." First Corinthians 16:23: "The grace of the Lord Jesus be with you." Second Corinthians 13:13: "The grace of the Lord Jesus Christ, beloved of God and the communion of the holy spirit be with all of you." Galatians 6:18: "May the grace of our Lord Jesus Christ be with your spirit. Amen." Ephesians 6:24: "Grace be with all who love the Lord Jesus Christ, in incorruption." Philippians 4:23: "The grace of the Lord Jesus Christ be with your spirit." Colossians 4:18: "I Paul, write this greeting with my own hand. Remember my chains. Grace be with you." First Thessalonians 5:28: "The grace of our Lord Jesus Christ be with you." Second Thessalonians 3:18: "The grace of our Lord Jesus Christ be with all of you." First Timothy 6:21: "Grace be with you." Second Timothy 4:22:

"Grace be with you." Titus 3:15: "Grace be with all of you." Philemon 25: "The grace of the Lord Jesus Christ be with your spirit. Amen." As you see, all letters of Paul end in a similar manner, which is similar to the salutation of the letter to the Hebrews.

THE LETTERS OF THE TRUE APOSTLES DO NOT END IN THIS MANNER. The name Timothy appears in the New Testament only in letters of Paul and also in the Acts of the Apostles; this name is not mentioned in Gospels or in the letters of the Apostles. Therefore this Timothy is strictly a member of Paul's group. Two letters of Paul are titled 1 and 2 Timothy. The letters of Paul that mention this name are Romans 16:21, 1 Corinthians 4:17 and 16:10; 2 Corinthians 1:1 and 19; Philippians 1:1 and 2:19; Colossians 1:1; 1 Thessalonians 1:1, 3:2 and 6; 2 Thessalonians 1:1; 1 Timothy 1:2 and 18, and 6:20; 2 Timothy 1:2; Philemon 1:1; the name also appears in Acts of the Apostles 16:1 and 3, 17:14, and 15, 18:5, 19:22, and 20:4.

Paul's satanic confession of faith is similar to his opinion or idea written in Ephesians 1:17 and 18: "I pray that the God of our Lord Jesus Christ, the Father of glory, may give you a spirit of wisdom and revelation as you come to know Him, illuminating the eyes of your heart," which refers to Satan who "opened the eyes" of the humans when he gave them "wisdom," according to Genesis 3:1–6. The expression in Hebrews 5:11 saying, "you need milk instead of solid food" is also written in the following letter of Paul, 1 Corinthians 3:2: "I fed you with milk, not solid food, for you were not ready for solid food." Hebrews 5:10–12 says: as a child who lacks "doctrine," it refers to Ephesians 4:14, which says, "we must no longer be children who fluctuate and are blown about by every wind of doctrine. . . ."

Other words or ideas contained in the letter to the Hebrews, which are typical of Paul in his other letters, are in: Ephesians 6:12, Romans 8:38 and 39, and 1 Corinthians 6:3 and

15:24. In these last two verses, he says, "You know that we will judge the angels" and "Then comes the end, when he hands over the kingdom to God the Father, after he has destroyed every ruler and every authority and power." Here again Paul lacks respect for angels, which is criticized by Peter in 2 Peter 2:10: "Specially those who indulge their flesh in depraved lust, and who despised authority." Hebrews 1:2: "But in these last days he has spoken to us by his Son, whom he appointed heir of all things"; this is similar to Galatians 4:7, which says, "So you are not longer a slave but a child, and if a child, then also an heir through God." This expression cannot be read in another book in the New Testament; it is typical and specific to Paul.

Hebrews 1:3 says, "He is the reflection of God's glory and the exact imprint of God's very being," similar to 1 Corinthians 11:7, which says, "since he is the image and reflection of God"; this expression also cannot be found in other books of the New Testament. Hebrews 3:12 mentions the words, "living God," which is an expression used by Paul in Romans 9:26, 2 Corinthians 3:3, and 6:16, and also in 1 Thessalonians 1:9. Hebrews 7:19 says, "For the law makes nothing perfect"; Hebrews 11:3, 4, 5, 7, 8, 9, and 11 say, "By the faith"; Hebrews chapter 12, verse 16 says, "Fornication," 13:17 says, "wake up." All these expressions and words (including the words "tribulation" and "grace") which are written in the Book of Hebrews, are typical of Paul and he used them frequently in his letters.

The repetition of word(s) and the use of antonyms within the same verse is part of the writing style of Paul. For example, Hebrews 4:10 says, "In his rest, also rest"; Hebrews 11:3 "from the invisible things have come the visible things". Hebrews 7:7, "It is beyond dispute that the inferior is blessed by the superior". 2 Corinthians 8:9, "Though he was rich . . . he became poor, so that by his poverty you might become rich". 2 Corinthians 8:13, "I do not mean that there should be relief for others and pressure on you." Philippians 4:12, "I know what it is to have little, and I know what it is to have plenty.... I have learned the secret of being well fed and of going hungry, of having plenty and of being in need." PAUL IS THE ONLY AUTHOR IN THE BIBLE WHO WRITES USING THIS STYLE. This is more proof that the letter to the Hebrews was written by Paul. The old debate about the real author of the letter to the Hebrews was created by those who wanted to avoid the criticism about Paul for writing the Satan's oath in Hebrews 5:10–13.

Other examples, which prove the same, are in Hebrews 5:10 and 2 Peter 3:16. Hebrews 5:10 says, "About this we have much to say that is hard to explain"; this verse was written by Paul and criticised by Peter, as written in 2 Peter 3:16 in which Peter says about Paul, ". . . speaking of this as he does in all his letters. There are some things in them HARD TO EXPLAIN"; other Bible translations say "of difficult intelligence" in both verses of Paul and Peter.

Paul despised the true apostles of Jesus Christ. Therefore it is not a surprise that the apostles answered him in a strong manner. Many versed in the letters of the apostles refer to Paul without mentioning his name, with the exception of Peter, who mentions Paul's name in 2 Peter 3:15. In James 1:23 and 24, James refers to Paul, who said that to be saved, we only need faith without works; "For if any are haters of the word and not doers, they are like those who look at themselves in a mirror, for they look at themselves and, on going away, immediately forget what they were like."

James 2:14, 17, 20, 24 and 26 say, "What good is it, my brothers, if you say you have faith but do not have works? Can faith save you? So faith by itself, if it has not works, is dead. Do you want to know . . . that faith apart from works is barren? You see that a person is justified by works and not by faith alone. For just as the body without the spirit is dead so faith without works is also dead." Therefore it is clear that Paul taught a doctrine that was opposed to the doctrine taught by the apostles of Christ. First John 3:18 says, "Little children, let us love, not in word or speech, but in truth and works." Peter is the apostle who said clearly that Paul was a Satanist; 2 Peter 3:15 and 16: "So also our beloved brother Paul wrote to you according to the WISDOM that was given to him. Speaking of this as he does in all his letters. There are some things in them hard to explain, which the ignorant and unstable twist to their own destruction, as they do to the other scriptures." Peter says there that Paul is a follower of the "WISDOM" tradition, and he also says that many men will destroy themselves by following the doctrine of Paul.

Peter continued, saying in 2 Peter 2:20–22: "For if, after they have escaped the defilements of the world through the knowledge of our Lord and Savior Jesus Christ, they are again entangled in them and overpowered, the last state has become worse for them than the first. For it will have been better for them never to have known the way of righteousness than, after knowing it, to turn back from the holy commandment that was passed on to them. It has happened to them according to the true proverb: The dog turns back to his own vomit, and the sow is washed only to wallow in the mud." This is a clear reference to Paul; there is no other person in the first century A.D. who fits the description, except Paul.

First John 2:18, 19, and 26 says, "Children, this is the last hour, and as you have heard that the Antichrist is coming, I say now that many antichrists have come, from this, we know that this is the last hour. THEY CAME FROM US, BUT THEY DON'T BELONG TO US." This refers to Paul, who was a Jew, but did not belong to the group of the apostles; verse 26 says, "I write these things to you concerning those who want to deceive you." First John 3:7 says, "Little children, let no one to deceive you," and the verse 4:3 says, "And every spirit that does not confess Jesus is not from God. And this is the spirit of the Antichrist, of which you have heard that it is coming, AND NOW IT IS ALREADY IN THE WORLD"; he is talking of Paul, who was already doing his anti-Christian work. Second Peter 2:1: "Like there were false prophets within the people, likewise will be false teachers among you, and they will introduce pernicious sects, they will even deny the Lord who rescued them, and will bring a sudden ruin on themselves."

Jude verse 4 says, "For some wicked man DISSIMU-LATELY have introduced among you, people who long ago were designated to this condemnation, who prevent the grace of our God into licentiousness." Using subtle lies, Paul introduced himself as a Trojan horse into the Christians. Jude 17, 18 and 19 say, "But you, beloved, must remember the predictions of the apostles of our lord Jesus Christ. They said to you that in the last time will be scoffers, indulging in their own ungodly lusts. THESE ARE THE WORLDLY PEOPLE, DEVOID OF THE SPIRIT, WHO ARE CAUSING DIVISIONS"; he is talking about Paul, who was causing division and schisms among the Christians. Second Peter 2:10–13 says, "Bold and willful, they are not afraid to blaspheme the authorities, whereas the angels, though greater in might and power, do not bring against them in slanderous judgment before the Lord. But these people are like irrational animals, they blaspheme about something they do not know. . . . They will be destroyed by their own corruption. . . . They are blots and blemishes, reveling in their dissipation while they feast with you."

This refers to Paul, who blasphemes about angels. The blasphemies about angels and authorities are in: Romans 8:38 and 39: "For I am convinced that neither death, nor life, nor angels, nor rulers, . . . will be able to separate us from the love of God"; 1 Corinthians 6:3: "Do you not know that we are to judge angels?"; 1 Corinthians 15:24: "Then comes the end, when he hands over the kingdom to God the Father, after he has destroyed every ruler and every authority"; Ephesians 6:12: "For our struggle is not against enemies of blood and flesh, but against the rulers, against the authorities"; also Colossians 2:9 and 10 speaks in the same manner about the authorities.

The "Holy Fathers" of the Catholic Church and other religious leaders of the Vatican throughout the ages have based their beliefs and works mainly on the writings of Paul, not only in the theological area, but also in some practical issues such as: the mass and collection carried out every Sunday (which was the first day of the week in the Jewish calendar). These were inspired in 1 Corinthians 16:2, which says, "On the first day of every week, each of you is to put aside and save what you consider convenient, so that collections need not to be taken when I come." Women should cover their heads during the mass, according to Paul, as written in 1 Corinthians 11:5 and 13, "But any woman who prays or prophesies with her head unveiled disgraces her head" and "Is it proper for a woman to pray to God with her head unveiled?" The concept of the bishop is based on words of Paul, according to Acts 20:28, "Keep watch over your service and over all the flock, over which the Holy Spirit has made you bishop to shepherd the church of God."

The permanence of the Jewish celebration of Pentecost among Christians is due to the work of Paul and Luke. This feast was a typical Jewish celebration, it was a remnant of the ancient paganism (the pagans celebrated this feast to honor the "goddess Mother-Earth"). Moses could not eliminate this feast because the Jewish people had a harsh heart, according to Exodus 23:16, "You shall observe the festival of harvest, of the first fruits of your labor, of what you sow in the field." Paul and Luke subtly introduced this feast among the Christians in Acts 2:1–3, "When the day of Pentecost had come, they were all together in one place. And suddenly from heaven there came a sound like the rush of a violent wind, and it filled the entire house where they were sitting. Divided tongues, as of fire, appeared among them, and a tongue rested on each of them." Paul and Luke made the Christian day of Pentecost coincide with the old Jewish feast, also called Pentecost. The "Fathers of the Church" created the concepts, creeds and rules which are the fundamental pillars or columns of the theology of the Vatican. Most of them lived during the first five centuries of this Christian Era. They are all defenders of the supposed holiness of David, Solomon, Jerusalem's temple, Paul, and the Doctrine of Wisdom. Some of these fathers were Augustine, Jerome, Basil, Origen, Cyril of Jerusalem, John Chrysostom, Athanasius, Dionysius the Areopagite, Leo the Great, Pope Gregory the Great, Lactantius, Clement of Alexandria, Fulgentius, Ambrose, Tertulian, Caesarius of Arles, Paulus Osorius, etc. Pope Gregory the Great (one of the fathers of the church) narrates in one of his "dialogues" a story in which "serpents" were killed by God, and God sent "birds" which took the "serpents" in their mouths and flew away. The secret satanic message in this story is the presence of the serpent together with a bird, which is the symbol for the plumed serpent (Satan) as can be seen in the forehead of the pharaohs, in the Mexican flag and in the American emblem (eagle with a band on its mouth, the band represents a serpent). Jerome, Origen, Pope Gregory the Great, Basil, Athanasius, and Cyril, clearly said that Jesus Christ is the "Wisdom" even knowing that Christ rejected the wisdom. All the Fathers of the Church used the concepts and phraseology of Paul. They were all satanists. Other savant pillars of the Vatican that defended the supposed holiness of David, Solomon, the Temple of Jerusalem, Paul and the Doctrine of Wisdom were Thomas Aquinas and Ignatius Loyola (the latter was the creator of the "Company of Jesus," also called the Jesuits).

The Freemasons also were inspired by Paul's writings to create some of their concepts. Remember that Freemasonry was created by satanic Jews; this is the reason that the Freemasons are acquainted with the writings of Paul. Galatians 2:9 says, "James, Cephas, and John who were considered the pillars recognized the grace that has been given to me; they gave to Barnabas and me the right hand as a sign of communion and fellowship." One of the most used symbols of the Freemason is the handshake; this greeting is also described by the Jewish writer Flavius Josephus in his book, *War of the Jews,* book 3 chapter 2, section 4, also chapter 8, sections 1, 4, and 5, and book 4, chapter 1, section 8, also book 6, chapter 6, section 2, and in others books where giving the "right hand" is a gesture-symbol, which means, "security" and "preservation." This gesture was used by the pagan Romans.

Paul and Josephus were both Pharisees; therefore they learned from the same theological sources. The Masons also ascribe the same meaning to the handshaking: "security" and "preservation" to their members. Actually, this is the reason why many Masons become members: they feel secure and they are helped by their "brothers" at the time of need, disgrace, or when they need a professional or political promotion (but also when they need a loan from a bank); they also preserve the life of a Mason when they are prisoners during a rebellion or a war.

The sacred Masonic concept of the "Great Architect of the Universe" (their 'Supreme Being," which is Satan) is inspired on the satanic tradition of the "wisdom" contained in the biblical Books of Wisdom (including the "Book of Wisdom" written by Solomon), in Paul's writing, and in the ideas of all the ancient builders of pyramids and temples. (Most probably the concept of "wisdom" and "dualism" were borne in Sumer and Egypt where satanism was first practiced). The Freemasons used the following biblical verses to strengthen their ideas:

Proverbs 8:12 and 30: "I, the WISDOM, have discretion with me; I possess the science and prudence," and "I was with Him as an ARCHITECT." Proverbs 9:1: "THE WISDOM HAS

BUILT HER HOUSE, SHE HAS HEWN HER SEVEN PIL-LARS." This refers to Solomon who built the temple of Jerusalem (this temple is the "house" with "seven pillars" of this verse). Remember that Solomon, who represents the "wisdom," is one of the spiritual fathers of the Masons. In Hebrews 11:10, Paul says: "For he wanted a city with strong foundations, whose ARCHITECT AND BUILDER IS GOD." Paul also says in 1 Corinthians 3:10, "According to the grace of God that was given to me, I, AS A WISE ARCHITECT, laid the foundations and some else is building on it." Paul is talking about the foundation or creation of his doctrine. The word "brother," used by the Masons to talk to each other, was taken from Paul's writing in which it is repeated seventy-seven times.

✿   ✿   ✿

Paul, according to the Apocalypse

Now I will demonstrate that the chapters 1,2 and 3 of the Book of Apocalypse have as a main goal to reveal the satanism of Paul. These chapters have the seven "letters" written by John to the "churches" of Asia. It should be remembered that *Apocalypse* is a Greek word, meaning "revelation," and "revelation" means to expose to the public light something that is hidden.

Apocalypse 1:4 says: "John, to the seven churches that are in Asia," refers to Asia Minor, which was the area where Paul focused his missionary works. Paul sent letters to many churches in Asia, which are his letters included in the New Testament. There are fourteen letters from Paul to the churches. John "sent" seven "letters" to the "churches," which is an expression of the ancient Jewish numerology. This is the first verse of the Apocalypse that refers to Paul. John knew that Paul frequently wrote letters to the churches in which he had followers. John was trying to get a manner of exposing the satanism of Paul without risking himself (John was a prisoner on the Island of Patmos). Then he decided to do it in a subliminal manner using confusing ideas in the Apocalypse. So he decided to "imitate" Paul, doing what Paul used to do: writing letters. The real intention of John was to pinpoint Paul, like a charade game. No one writes seven letters and puts them all together in a book instead of sending them to the different destinations. Therefore the seven letters are not real letters but sections of a book written with the intention of revealing the identity of Paul.

Apocalypse 1:4 also says: "Grace to you and peace from him who is and who was and who is to come, and from the seven spirits who are before his throne." Here John wants to pinpoint Paul, using words that Paul frequently used in his letters. "Grace" and "peace" are salutation words used by Paul at the beginning of all his letters, except the letter to the Hebrews. Let us see those letters:

Romans 1:7: "Grace to you and peace from God."
1 Corinthians 1:3: "Grace to you and peace from God."
2 Corinthians 1:2: "Grace to you and peace from God."
Galatians 1:3: "Grace to you and peace from God."
Ephesians 1:2: "Grace to you and peace from God."
Philippians 1:2: "Grace to you and peace from God."
Colossians 1:2: "Grace to you and peace from God."
1 Thessalonians 1:2: "Grace to you and peace."
2 Thessalonians 1:2: "Grace to you and peace from God."
1 Timothy 1:2: "Grace, mercy and peace from God."
2 Timothy 1:2: "Grace, mercy and peace from God."
Titus 1:4: "Grace and peace from God."
Philemon 3: "Grace to you and peace from God."

Apocalypse 1:5: "the first born of the dead" refers to Colossians 1:18, which says, "he is the beginning, the first born of the dead."

Apocalypse 1:5: "the ruler of the kings of the earth" refers to Colossians 2:10: he "is the head of every ruler and authority."

Apocalypse 1:6: "and he made us kings and priests of God" is based on Hebrews 5:5 and 6, and 7:1: "So also Christ . . . in becoming a high priest. . . . He says also in another place "You are a priest forever, according to the order of Melchizedec," "This King Melchizedec, of Salem, priest of Most High God." Paul used frequently the word "priest," John knew this and for this reason, he used the word in this verse (because he was thinking in Paul).

Apocalypse 1:10: "I was in the spirit on the DAY OF THE LORD" is based on 1 Corinthians 1:8: "You may be blameless ON THE DAY OF OUR LORD JESUS CHRIST." The "day of the Lord" is mentioned also by Paul in 1 Corinthians 5:5, 2 Corinthians 1:14, 1 Thessalonians 5:2, and 2 Thessalonians 2:2.

Apocalypse 1:11: "Write in a book what you see and send it to the seven churches: to Ephesus, to Smyrna, to Pergamum, to Thyatira, to Sardis, to Philadelphia, and to Laodicea." Ephesus is mentioned in all the Bible only by Paul, Luke, and in this verse of the Apocalypse. Ephesus is mentioned by Luke in Acts 18:19, 21 and 24, in 19:1, 17, 26 and 35, and in 20:16 and 17; by Paul in 1 Corinthians 15:32 ("I fought with wild animals in Ephesus"), in 1 Corinthians 16:8 ("I will stay in Ephesus until Pentecost"), also in Ephesians 1:1, 1 Timothy 1:3 and in 2 Timothy 1:18 and 4:12. The city of Thyatira is mentioned in all the Bible in this apocalyptic verse and in Acts 16:14 when speaking about the trip of Paul to Europe it says: "A certain woman named Lydia, a worshiper of God, from the city of THYATIRA, was listening carefully to us. The Lord had opened her heart to listen to what PAUL was saying." In this last verse, we can clearly see the scriptural style of John: he tries to identify or pinpoint a person, mentioning word(s) and/or facts that are somehow related to that person. In this specific case, John knew that in the same verse where the word "Thyatira" was, the word

"Paul" was also present. The city of Laodicea is mentioned in the Bible only in this apocalyptic verse and in the letter of Paul to the Colossians 2:1, and 4:13, 15, and 16.

Apocalypse 2:1: "To the angel of the church in Ephesus," the comment is the same as in the previous paragraph.

Apocalypse 2:2 and 3: "I know your works, your patience, and that you can not tolerate evildoers, YOU HAVE TESTED THOSE WHO CLAIM TO BE APOSTLES, BUT ARE NOT, AND HAVE FOUND THEM TO BE LIARS; and you have patience, and suffered for the sake of my name." All these ideas lead to Paul. For example: 1 Corinthians 16:10: "If Timothy goes there, see that he has nothing to fear among you, for he is doing the WORK of the Lord just like me"; the "works" of Paul are also mentioned in Acts 13:2, 14:26, and 15:38, in 1 Corinthians 4:12, Ephesus 4:12, Philippians 1:6, 1 Thessalonians 2:9, 2 Thessalonians 3:8, and 1 Timothy 4:10. About the suffering of Paul, 2 Corinthians 11:27 says: "In toil and hardship, through many a sleepless night, hungry and thirsty, often without food, cold and naked." 2 Corinthians 11:16–23 also speaks about the works and sufferings of Paul. The "patience" John refers to is the patience of Paul, as we read in Romans 8:25: "But if we hope for what we do not see, we wait for it with patience"; also in 2 Corinthians 6:4, 2 Timothy 3:10, 2 Corinthians 12:12, and in Hebrews 6:12. John says "You can tolerate the evildoers." This refers to Romans 12:9, also "Let love be genuine, hate what is evil," and Romans 12:21: "Do not be overcome by evil"; Philippians 3:2 says "Beware of the evil workers." There are more verses that I can mention on all this topics, but I chose some of them as examples. In the verse of the Apocalypse that we are analyzing, John says, "Those who claim to be apostles, but they are not." He is clearly speaking about Paul. I say this because besides the true apostles of Christ, Paul IS THE ONLY ONE IN THE BIBLE WHO CLAIMS TO BE AN APOSTLE, and as I have already proved, he was not a man of God, but a Satanist. In the following verses, we see that Paul claims to be an apostle:

1 Corinthians 9:1: "Am I not free? Am I not an apostle? Have I not seen Jesus our Lord?" Paul never saw Jesus; he said that he "heard" the voice of Jesus when Christ appeared to him on his way to Damascus; Christ himself chose the true apostles.

Romans 1:1: "Paul, a servant of Jesus Christ, called to be an apostle, chosen to proclaim the gospel of God." I said that Paul was not selected by Jesus; he is the one who lied when he said that Jesus talked to him (years after Jesus was killed) in a kind of vision.

Romans 11:13: "As long as I am an apostle of the Gentiles, I will honor my ministry."

1 Corinthians 1:1: "Paul, called to be an apostle of Christ Jesus by the will of God."

2 Corinthians 1:1: "Paul, an apostle of Christ Jesus by the will of God."

2 Corinthians 12:11: "for I am not at all inferior to the other apostles."

Galatians 1:1: "Paul, neither an apostle of men nor by men, but through Jesus Christ and God the Father."

Ephesians 1:1: "Paul, an apostle of Christ Jesus by the will of God."

Colossians 1:1: "Paul, an apostle of Christ Jesus by the will of God."

1 Thessalonians 2:7: I "might exercise on you my authority as an apostle of Christ."

1 Timothy 1:1: "Paul, an apostle of Christ Jesus by the command of God our Savior."

2 Timothy 1:1: "Paul, an apostle of Christ by the will of God."

Titus 1:1: "Paul, a servant of God and an apostle of Jesus Christ."

Apocalypse 2:4: "But I have this against you, that you have abandoned the love you had at first." This refers to Paul, this verse means: you, Paul, are a person who changed, before you were diferent, before you persecuted Christians, your first loves were for the leaders of the Judaism, for those who killed Christ.

Apocalypse 2:5: "Consider then from what YOU HAVE FALLEN." This refers to Paul, who said that on his way to Damascus he heard the voice of Jesus and for that he fell to the ground and then became a Christian. This is written in Acts 9:1–4: Paul saw a "light from the sky around him" and then "he fell to the ground and heard a voice saying to him: Saul, Saul, why do you persecute me?" Acts 26:13 and 14 repeat this same story.

Apocalypse 2:6: "Yet this is to your credit: you hate the works of the Nicolaitans, which I also hate"; the Bible only mention Nicolaus in Acts 6:5: "and they chose Stephen, a man full of faith and the Holy Spirit, together with Philip, Prochorus, Nicanor, Timon, Parmenas, and Nicolaus, a proselyte of Antioch"; Antioch was one of the places closely related to Paul. These men are mentioned there by Luke (the author of Acts) who was part of the group of Paul. Therefore, John mentioned the "Nicolaitans" because in the same verse where "Nicolaus" appeared also Paul is present (through his association with Antioch).

Apocalypse 2:7: "To the conqueror I will give him permission to eat of the tree of life, which is in the paradise of my God." John knew that Paul "ate" not of the tree of life, but of the tree of the "science" of good and evil, as Paul said in Hebrews 5:10–13.

Apocalypse 2:9: "I know your tribulation and poverty, even though you are rich. I know the blasphemy of those who say that they are Jews, but they are not; THEY ARE THE SYNAGOGUE OF SATAN." This is a terrible and interesting verse and at the same time very clear. John knew about the satanism of Paul and other Judaists, including the high authorities of the Temple of Jerusalem (the Temple of Solomon) and the synagogues, for this reason John called them "the synagogue of Satan." The Judaists killed Christ; a result of this murder was that the follower of Christ reinforced the rupture from the Judaists and their practices, including attending the temple and synagogues. But Paul continued attending synagogues after his "conversion" to Christianism, as we can see in the following verses: Acts 14:1: Paul and Barnabas "went into the Jewish synagogue" and made a speech and many new converts; Acts 13:13 and 14: "Paul and his companions . . . went into the synagogue on the sabbath day and sat down"; something similar can be read in Acts 9:2 and 20; 17:1, 10 and 17; 13:5; 15:21; and 18:4, 7, 8, 19 and 26.

Apocalypse 2:10: "Beware, the devil is about to throw some of you into PRISON, so that you may be tested, AND YOU WILL HAVE A TRIBULATION OF TEN DAYS"; here the key elements to decipher the puzzle are: "prison," "tribulation," and "ten days." These three data refer to Paul, according to the following verses: Acts 24:27 and 25:1 and 6: ". . . After two years had passed, Felix was succeeded by Porcius Festus; and since he wanted to grant the Jews a favor, Felix LEFT PAUL IN PRISON," and then "Festus went to the province. . . . Having been with them about eight or TEN days, he went to Caesarea, and the next day he was seated on his tribunal and ordered Paul to be brought." I previously mentioned other verses speaking about Paul's tribulations.

Apocalypse 2:13: "I know where you are living, WHERE SATAN'S THRONE IS, but you still keep my name, and did not deny my faith even in the days of ANTIPAS, my witness, my faithful one, who was KILLED AMONG YOU where Satan lives." The key elements to decipher the puzzle are: "the throne of Satan," "you keep my name," "you did not deny my faith," "Antipas," "my witness," "my faithful one," "was killed among you" and "where Satan lives." David, Solomon, and their follow-ers were and are Satanists, and their main temple (the Temple of Solomon, which is the Temple of Jerusalem) is the "throne of Satan." "You keep my name and did not deny my faith," refers to Paul who said to be a Christian and have faith. "Anti-pas" refers to HEROD ANTIPAS, the tetrarch who was the ruler of Jerusalem WHEN JESUS CHRIST WAS KILLED in A.D. 33. "My witness, my faithful one" refers to Christ, as we can see in these verses: Apocalypse 1:5: "Jesus Christ, the faithful witness," Apocalypse 3:14: "This says the Amen, the faithful and true witness, the origin of God's creation," and Apocalypse 19:11: "I saw a heaven opened, and there was a white horse, and his rider is called Faithful and True, and in righteousness he judges." "Was killed among you" refers to Christ, who was killed by the Jews. This verse speaks about Paul and the rest of the satanic Jews. So this verse (Apocalypse 2:13) really means: I know where you lived, I know you lived in Jerusalem, where the Temple of Solomon is, which is the Satan's throne, I know you were not God's follower although you said that you had faith in Christ, and I also know that at the time of Herod Antipas, the Jews killed Jesus Christ (my faithful witness) among you in Jerusalem where Satan lives.

Apocalypse 2:14: "But I have something against you: you tolerate those who follow the doctrine of Balaam, who taught Balak to put a stumbling block before the people of Israel, to eat food sacrificed to idols and practice fornication." The bibli-cal book of Numbers, chapters 22, 23 and 24, speak about Ba-laam and Balak; Balak (a Moabite King) and other Moabite princes tried to curse Israel with the help of Balaam, who at the end did not want to help. Paul tried to do the same: deviate Israel from the right pathway. But the important and key ele-ments in this verse are "to eat food sacrificed to idols" and "fornication," which are issues that Paul described abundantly in his letters. For example, 1 Corinthians 6:13: "The body is not for fornication, but for the Lord"; "fornication" means to worship idols. Galatians 5:19 and 20 say "Now, the works of the flesh are obvious: fornication, impurity. . . ." Ephesians 5:3 and 5 say, "About fornication . . . must not even be mentioned that it exists among you" and ". . . no fornicator or impure person . . . has any inheritance in the kingdom of Christ." About fornication in the letters of Paul, read Colossians 3:5, Acts 21:25 (the Book of Luke), 1 Corinthians 6:18, 1 Thessalonians 4:3, and Hebrews 13:4. Paul speaks about eating of the food sacrificed to the idols in 1 Corinthians 8:1: "About the food sacrificed to idols, we know that we all possess science" and 8:10 says "Do not consider himself induced to eat of the food sacrificed to the idols?"

Apocalypse 2:17: "To everyone who conquers I will give them some of the hidden manna." Paul speaks about the manna in Hebrews 9:3 and 4: "There was a golden glass which contains the manna." Paul said here that there was manna in the ark, which is not true (the word *manna* appears in the Bible eighteen times. There is no indication that there was manna in the ark); for this reason John called this nonexistent manna of Paul: the "hidden manna."

Apocalypse 2:18: "To the angel of the church of Thyatira write . . .", I already said that in acts of the Apostles 16:14 appears the name Thyatira together with the name of Paul. (The name Thyatira appears in the Bible only in these two verses.)

Apocalypse 2:19: "I know your works, your love, your faith, your ministry, your patience and your last works, which are greater than the first." I already spoke about this when analyzing Apocalypse 2:2.

Apocalypse 2:20: "But I have this against you: you allow Jezebel, who calls herself a prophet, who is teaching and beguiling my servants to make them practice fornication and to eat food sacrificed to idols." Jezebel was a pagan daughter of a Phoenician king of Sidon. She made the Israelites worship the god Baal, according to 1 Kings 16:31, 18:4, and others, including 2 Kings chapter 9. Paul speaks abundantly about fornication, as I said. "That woman who calls herself a prophet" applied to Paul who considered himself an apostle. So Apocalypse 2:20 really says: "But I have against you that you allow Paul, who calls himself apostle, to teach and deceive my servants and make them to eat of the food sacrificed to the idols" (In 1 Corinthians 10:19 and 25 Paul approved of eating food sacrificed to the idols).

Apocalypse 2:21: "I have given him time to repent, but he doesn't want to repent of his fornication," is talking about Paul.

Apocalypse 2:22: "I am throwing her in a bed, and those who commit adultery with her, in great tribulation, unless they repent of their works." Here the key elements are: bed, tribulation, and works. Acts 28:8 say, "The father of Publius lay sick in bed. . . . Paul came to him . . . and cured him." I have already analyzed the "tribulations" and "works" of Paul.

Apocalypse 2:24: "And to you, the rest of Thyatira, those who don't follow that doctrine, those who do not know the deep things of Satan, I do not lay on you any other burden." This refers to Paul, who says in 1 Corinthians 2:10: "For the Spirit searches everything, even the deep things of God."

Apocalypse 3:1: "You have a name of being alive, but you are dead." This refers to Paul, who was already dead when John wrote the Apocalypse around the year A.D. 96.

Apocalypse 3:3: "If you don't wake up"; (the Bible in Spanish says "*velar*"). This is an expression typical of Paul, as in Acts 20:31, 1 Corinthians 16:13, and Colossians 4:2.

Apocalypse 3:5: "I will confess your name before my Father" is based on Romans 10:9 and Philippians 2:11 (here it says "and every tongue should confess that Jesus Christ is Lord").

Apocalypse 3:14: "To the angel of the church of Laodicea write . . . ," the name of this city is only in the Bible in this verse and in the letter of Paul to the Colossians 2:1, 4:13, 15, and 16.

Apocalypse 3:18: "I advise you to buy from me gold refined by fire . . . and salve to anoint YOUR EYES SO THAT YOU MAY SEE." It refers to Paul who became temporarilty blind after "seeing" the light from the sky and "heard" Jesus on the day of his supposed conversion. This is written in Acts 9:8, 9, 12, 17, and 18, where they say, "Saul rose us from the ground, and having his EYES OPENED HE COULD NOT SEE. He was taken to Damascus, where he spent three days without seeing, eating, and drinking. . . . Saul saw a man in a vision named Ananias, who went in and laid his hand on Saul and he recovered." Later Ananias went to the house where Paul was and told him, "Brother Saul, the Lord Jesus, who appeared to you on your way here, has sent me so that you may regain your sight. And immediately something like scales fell from his eyes, and his sight was restored."

With these biblical verses, I have demonstrated that John tried to expose the hidden satanism of Paul. There are other verses in the Apocalypse speaking in the same tenor, but I do not mention them for reasons of space.

16. The Satanism of Luke

I previously said that the possibility exists that the writings of Luke (the gospel and Acts of the Apostles) were in reality written by Paul. Luke is the person who narrated in Acts of the Apostles the supposed conversion of Paul, so Luke is co-responsible for the introduction of Paul into Christianity with the intention of perverting Christianity. This Book of Luke contains many of Paul's opinions; Luke made him speak in the first person frequently. In chapter 1 of the "gospel of "Luke," the appearance of an angel in the Temple of Jerusalem is narrated; this angeology was one of the preferred topics of Paul: the angels and the holiness of the temple. In a former chapter, we read a verse in which Paul says that the Apostles of Christ continued to attend the temple after the death of Jesus, which should not be believed because Christ broke with the belief and practices of Judaism (including the belief in the holiness of the temple). Luke also believed in the holiness of the temple: according to the gospel of Luke 24:53, he said that after the ascension of Christ to heaven, the apostles, "were continually in the temple blessing God." The angel, who according to the gospel of Luke appeared in the temple, was Gabriel, the same angel that Muhammad said appeared to him and took him to the Temple of Jerusalem. The appearance of this angel in the temple is only narrated by Luke, it is not in the other gospels. The appearance and relation of this angel with the temple is a lie of the satanic Luke and Muhammad, with the intention to make us believe in the holiness of the Temple of Jerusalem, as

David and Solomon did. Making us believe in the holiness of the temple forced us to believe also in the holiness of David and Solomon, and this is the goal of Luke, Paul, and Muhammad.

Luke, like Paul, made a eulogy to David, according to the following verses: Luke 1:27: ". . . to a virgin engaged to a man whose name was Joseph, of the House of David." Luke 1:31 and 32: "You will conceive in your womb and bear a son, and you will name him Jesus . . . and the Lord God will give to him the throne of David, his father." Verses 1:46–56 contain the song of Mary, which is inspired in the Davidian Psalms. This song of Mary is the famous "Magnificat," adored by the Vatican. In the verses 2:4 and 11, 3:32, and 18:38, Luke also mentions and adores David.

In the following verses, we will see the opinion of Luke about the satanic tradition of "wisdom." (We have to remember that all the books of the Old Testament are grouped in three different parts, in order of appearance: the Books of the Law, the Books of Wisdom, and the Books of the Prophets). Luke 2:40 says of Jesus Christ when he was a child, "The child grew and became strong, filled with wisdom," which is a blasphemy because we know and Luke knew that Christ rejected the "wisdom." Luke 2:52 says, "And Jesus increased in wisdom and in years." Luke 11:49 says, "Therefore also the wisdom of God said: I will send them prophets and apostles." These are words of Christ according to Luke, which should not be believed. Luke 21:15 states some words supposedly ascribed to Jesus: "I will give you words and a wisdom that none of your opponents will be able to withstand or contradict." Luke 24:44 also shows that Luke was a Satanist. This verse says that Christ said, "These are my words that I spoke to you while I was still with you: that everything written about me IN THE LAW OF MOSES, THE PROPHETS, AND THE PSALMS must be fulfilled." This is a lie of Luke because he knew perfectly well that Jesus Christ only approved the "Law and the Prophets" and rejected the

Book of Wisdom (including some Psalms that are satanic like the Davidian Psalms). The gospels of Matthew and John say that Christ approved only the "Law and the Prophets." Mark does not mention the topic.

In the following verses, we will see that Christ only approved the "Law and the Prophets." In Matthew 5:17, Christ said, "Do not think that I have come to abolish the Law or the Prophets." In Matthew 7:12 Christ said, "In everything do to others as you would have them do to you, for this is the Law and the Prophets." In Matthew 11:13, Christ says, "for all the prophets and the Law prophesied until John came." Matthew 22:40: Christ said, "On these two commandments hang all the Law and the prophets." In John 1:45, Christ said, "Philip found Nathanael and said to him: we have found him about whom Moses in the Law and the Prophets wrote, Jesus, son of Joseph from Nazareth." JESUS CHRIST NEVER SAID, "THE LAW, THE PROPHETS, AND THE BOOK OF WISDOM," a clear indication that he rejected the Book of Wisdom. (We should know that not all of the Psalms are satanic, even though they were written by Davidian *and/or* Solomonic Satanists; the same thing happened with the Egyptian and Mayan Satanists; they composed poems that were not satanic. Also the Book of Wisdom has several chapters that are not satanic.)

Luke is the only Evangelist who depicted Mary (the mother of Jesus) with a veneration to the point of a fanatic exaltation; the Vatican gets inspiration from Luke in order to practice the fanatical and absurd "Mariology," which is the worship of the Virgin Mary as a spiritual and invisible entity with angelic characteristics or supernatural power. Millions of Christians have substituted Christ for the worship of the Virgin Mary. This can be seen in family altars and public processions.

The "Beatitudes" (the Blessings) are narrated by Matthew in 5:3–11 and by Luke in 6:20–23, but Luke adds the condemnation of Christ to the sinners in 6:24–26; here Luke shows his cynicism and double-face because he knew that Christ is love and forgiveness and not condemnation. In a previous chapter, we saw that Paul said that Peter killed two persons (in the Acts of the Apostles). Luke also displayed the same cynicism and negative attitude when saying that James and John proposed to Christ that they should kill several persons, according to Luke 9:51 and 54, which say, "when the days drew near for him to be taken up, he set his face to go to Jerusalem. When his disciples James and John saw it, they said: Lord, do you want us to command fire to come down from heaven and consume them?" This story is only in the gospel of Luke; it is not in the other true evangelists' books, so we should not believe this story.

Here ends this analysis of the satanism of Luke. With these verses that I have mentioned, I proved that Luke followed the wisdom tradition, and that most probably Luke is the same person as Paul or that the writings of Luke are in reality the writings of Paul; some scholars prefer to believe that Luke wrote with his own hand the ideas and teachings of Paul.

17. The Satanism of Muhammad and the Koran

Millions of human beings were and are followers of the Islamic religion since the time this religion appeared in the seventh century of the Christian era. Millions of Muslims have died in battles and wars, fighting against the unbeliever and sometimes among themselves, in internal war. They believe that Muhammad was a man chosen by God to lead humans to the right pathway. Muhammad said that the Angel Gabriel dictated the contents of the Koran to him. I will explain how Muhammad deceived his followers and why millions of Muslims died and continue to die today in wars under the belief that they are defending the Law of God.

To understand the true meaning of the Koran, it is necessary to know the real meaning of the Apocalypse. Reading the Bible carefully, you can understand the deep and sometimes hidden meaning of facts, narration, and human personalities who played an important role in this book. Also in order to understand the meaning of the Koran, it was necessary for me to study for about nine years, the history, politics, and religion of ancient and modern civilizations.

I have already proved that David, Solomon, and Paul were Satanists. I proved it by using the Bible. We cannot understand the Koran if we do not understand the Bible. The satanism of the rebel Jews who made human sacrifices in the Valley of Ben-Hinon, in Israel, continued subtly in the Koran. The Muslim religion is not a new and different religion; it is a continuation of the Davidian satanism. The Koran is a mere commentary on several books of the Bible. Let us discuss more details about this.

The Jews of Arabia were waiting for the arrival of a great prophet of Judaism, who was to appear in the seventh century A.D. When Muhammad was presented as that great prophet, many Jews of Arabia accepted him until Muhammad started showing ambition and independence. The obscure persons who taught Muhammad were Jewish; among them was Waraqa. Muhammad married Kadija, who was a rich Jewish widow. At that time Muhammad was an unknown and unimportant person. As soon as Muhammad started prophesying, he started saying that he was a descendant of Abraham, which made people think that Muhammad was a Jew. He also said that the Arabians were also descendants of Abraham through Ishmael, a son of Abraham. This assertion concerning his genealogy has not been proved. To say that he is a descendant of Abraham is a clear proof of his Judaism through his physical-racial heritage or by his religious feelings in favor of Judaism. Other details that show his Judaism are: the respect for the Sabbath (to rest on Saturday) which is one of the most typical and fanatical Jewish practices; this is written in the Koran, Sura (chapter) 2:61 (the number after the colon is the verse) and 4:50. The last one says, "We have cursed those who violated the Sabbath"; also not to eat pork as we can read in the verse 2:168, which says, "It is forbidden for you to eat of dead animals, blood, or the meat of pork"; also the verses 5:4, 6:146, and 16:116 repeat the prohibition not to eat pork.

These teachings were extracted from the Pentateuch, which are the first five books of the Bible. At the beginning of his religious activities, Muhammad practiced Kebla (the revelation or sacred genuflecting) and he did it toward the direction of Jerusalem, but then after becoming an enemy of the Jews, he changed the direction of Kebla toward Mecca where the "sacred stone" of the Arabian pagans was, they have worshiped this stone from time immemorial. This sacred genuflecting in which the person "fell upon their face" is also a Jewish practice, according to Ezekiel 43:3 and 44:4. Another Jewish practice that Muhammad imitated was circumcision; it is believed that Muhammad was born circumcised, of course, a false belief.

Another example of the Judaism of Muhammad is his own opinion that the Koran was dictated to him by the angel Gabriel, an angel who is part of Jewish theology (Gabriel is mentioned by Luke, but not by the other Evangelists). Muhammad also said that the Koran was also dictated to him in order to "corroborate" the Jewish Scriptures, as we can read in the following verses. (Readers should know that different translations of the Koran have a variation in the numbering of verses; for example, verse 2:38 in one book is 2:40 in other; I use the numbering that was used in *The Koran,* translated to Spanish by Joaquin Garcia Bravo, which publisher was "Edicomunicacion S.A.," Spain, the year 1986, but I am not quoting this book or any other translation.)

Koran, Sura 2:38: "Oh children of Israel! Remember the favours I have given to you; fulfill the part of your covenant, and I will fulfill my part; believe in the book that I sent you TO CORROBORATE your Scriptures; don't be the first in denying your belief, and don't part with my signs for a trifling price."

Sura 2:83: "When they received from God A BOOK CONFIRMING THEIR SCRIPTURES (before they asked God for a victory against the unbelievers), this book that was announced before, they did not believe on it. The curse of Allah is on disbelievers."

Sura 2:85: "And when it is said to them: believe in what God sent you from above, they answered: We believe in what has been sent to us from above; and they don't believe in what came after that; and, nonetheless, THIS BOOK CONFIRMS THEIR SCRIPTURES. Tell them: if you have faith, why have you killed the messengers of the Lord?"

131

Sura 2:91: "Say: Who is an enemy to Gabriel? He is the one who, with the authorization of God, deposited in your heart the BOOK DESTINED TO CONFIRM THE SACRED BOOKS before it, to be a guide and to announce new happy things to the believers." The important concepts in these Suras are "son of Israel," "faithful to my covenant," "corroborate your Scriptures," "killed the messengers of God," and "Gabriel." All these concepts are pure Judaism.

Sura 2:95: "When the apostles came to them (sent by God), CONFIRMING THEIR SACRED BOOKS, one part of those who received the Scriptures put them behind their backs as if they didn't know it." "One part of those . . ." refers to the Christians who rejected the Book of Wisdom; we will see this in other verses.

Sura 3:2: "He has sent you with all true THE BOOK THAT CONFIRMS WHAT WAS SENT BEFORE; he has sent from above the Pentateuch and the Gospel to guide mankind. He has sent THE DISTINCTION." This "distinction" refers to the satanic oath of Genesis 3:1–6, which teaches to know ("distinguish") between good and evil. Sura 2:181 has the Muhammad satanic confession of faith, as we will see.

Sura 4:50: "You who have received the scriptures, believe in what God has sent you from heaven TO CONFIRM YOUR SACRED BOOKS, before we erase the gestures of your faces and turn them to the opposite side. Believe before we curse you as we cursed those who violated the Sabbath; the order of God was immediately fulfilled." Note in this verse the defense of Muhammad of the Jewish Sabbath.

Sura 46:11: "The Book of Moses existed before the Koran; it was given to be a guide to mankind and as a proof of the mercy of God. THE KORAN WAS SENT TO CONFIRM THE BOOK OF MOSES IN ARABIAN LANGUAGE, as a warning to the evildoers and to teach the righteous happy new things."

Other Suras that say almost the same are: 5:52, 6:92, 10:38, 12:111 and 46:29. As you can read clearly, the Koran is pure Judaism. There is not in the Koran a new theological concept (s). The Koran claims to be a book that speaks the truth; the same thing was said by the criminal Aztecs in some of their codices (books), so we should not judge the Koran and/or the Aztecs by what they said about themselves. These are all the verses in which the Koran says that it was sent from God "to corroborate the old Jewish Scriptures"; there are thirteen verses about it, which means that this idea is important in the Koran.

A careful study of the Koran shows that 34.7% (2,326) of the verses are copied, based, or closely related to the Bible; the rest 65.3% (3,894) verses are not directly related to the Bible. But none of the last have a new IMPORTANT theological concept. The verses in the Koran containing theological ideas that are not in the Bible (but lack importancy) are: 2:27, 28, 29, 30, 31 and 32, 96, 185, 5:34, 6:100, 128, 130, 7:10 through 17, 23, 39, 44, 171, 9:36, 11:9, 13:12, 15:31 through 42, 41:11, 43:77, 50:16 and 17, 20, 72:1, 82:10 and 11, 97:1 through 4, and few others. The verses 7:10 through 17 and 15:31 through 42 speak about the rebellion of Satan and his angels, which is a topic beloved by the Jews according to their tradition.

Another important issue in which Muhammad displays that he was a follower of the Judaism is the dispute between Jews and Christians concerning theology and biblical matters. In this dispute Muhammad took part in favor of the Judaists, as we can see in the following verses.

Sura 3:101: "Do not be like those who after being witness of evident signs have divided themselves and have a dispute among them, for they will suffer a cruel punishment." Muhammad never made a miracle or other "sign," so these signs are those narrated in the Bible.

Sura 42:11: "He has established for you a religion that he recommended to Noah; it is the one revealed to you, Oh

Muhammad, it is the one we recommended to Abraham, to Moses, and to Jesus saying: Keep this religion, do not divide yourselves into sects."

Sura 45:15 and 16: "We have given THE PENTATEUCH, THE WISDOM AND THE PROPHETS TO THE SONS OF ISRAEL; we gave them excellent things for food and favoured them above all men." This last expression "we favoured them above all men" is repeated in other verses, which also proved that Muhammad was a Judaist. Verse 16 says, "They didn't start dividing themselves until after the science was given to them . . . your Lord will decide about their dispute." MUHAMMAD AP-PROVED IN VERSE 45:15 THE BELIEF IN THE "LAW (THE PENTATEUCH WHICH ARE THE LAWS OF MO-SES), THE WISDOM AND THE PROPHETS" in clear contradiction to Jesus Christ who only approved "the Law and the Prophets," as I previously showed.

Other verses speaking about the "dispute" between the Christians and the Jews are: 2:171, 209, 254, 3:17, 22, 39, 47, 48, 58 and 59; 4:68; 5:53; 10:93; 11:112; 13:14; 16:29, 66, 125, 27:78; 32:25; 40:58, 71, 41:45; 42:8, 13 and 33; 43:63 and 65.

Closely related to the topic of the dispute between Christians and Jews is the opinion of Muhammad about those Israelites who distorted the Jewish Scripture. For instance: Sura 2:25: "The perverts who broke the covenant of the Lord (concluded before) and separated what God ordered to be kept together, and made mischief in the earth, those are the unfortunate." Muhammad is talking here about Christ and his followers who eliminated ("separated") the belief in the satanic Books of Wisdom of the Bible.

Sura 2:70: "Now, Oh Muslims! Do you wish that the Israelites become believers. . . . Some of them obeyed the word of God, but later they altered it after they understood it, and they knew it well."

Sura 2:100: "We do not eliminate any verse from this book nor will we erase one verse from your memory."

Sura 2:169: "Those who occult part of the book sent from above . . . fill their belly with fire."

Other verses that speak about the contradictions between Jews and Christians, and the elimination of the belief in part of the Scriptures are: 1:7, 2:13, 15, 39, 56, 73, 94, 134, 141 and 154, 207; 3:5, 19, 20, 22, 62, 64 and 72, 4:47, 5:16, and 76 through 81.

✿   ✿   ✿

The Koran contains other strong blasphemy against Christ. Muhammad accused the Christians of worshiping divinities with God, which is an attack on a fundamental belief of the Christians: monotheism. Muhammad also said that Christ is a liar and a false messenger of God.

Sura 5:76: "Unbeliever is the one who says: God is the Messiah, son of Mary. Did not say the Messiah that about himself: O sons of Israel! Love your God, who is your and my Lord? To those who associate God with other gods, God will forbid them the entrance to the garden, and their house will be the fire. The perverts should not wait for mercy." We see clearly that Muhammad called Christ and his followers "perverts."

Sura 2:20: "Do not associate companions with God."

Sura 3:57: "Tell the Jews and the Christians: O people of the Scriptures! Come to listen to one word; let everything be equal between you and us; let's agree in that we will not worship other gods than God and that we will associate nothing with him."

Sura 4:51: "God does not forgive that we associate other gods with him . . . those who associate God with other creatures commit an enormous sin." Here Muhammad condemns the Christians because they considered Christ as the son of God.

Sura 5:116: "Then, God told Jesus: Have you said to the mankind: Take my mother and me for gods beside the only God? For your glory, not! HOW CAN I SAY WHAT IS NOT TRUE?"

Sura 6:70: "Will we go over our footsteps after God conducted us by the right pathway, SIMILAR TO THAT ONE THAT THE DEMONS MISLAID IN THE DESERT." It refers to Christ who was tempted in the desert by Satan.

Sura 9:31: "They have taken their wise men and monks, and to the Messiah, son of Mary, instead of God, as their Lord."

Other verses on the same topics are in: 2:21, 2:160, 3:144, 4:40, 4:116, 6:137, 149, 151 and 152; 7:31, 9:31, 10:19, 29, 67, 104, 105 and 106; 11:57 and 103; 12:38 and 40:13–17 and 33; 14:35, 15:96, 16:1, 3, 20, 37 and 56.

❉   ❉   ❉

David, Solomon, and Paul believed in the satanic confession of faith as I proved before. Muhammad did the same in the following verses of the Koran:

Sura 2:181 (Sura 2–185 in other Koran): "The month of Ramadan, during which the Koran descended from above to guide mankind, to be a clear explanation of the precepts, and TO DISTINGUISH BETWEEN GOOD AND EVIL; that is the time for fasting." He is clearly talking about the precepts taught to Eve by the Serpent, according to Genesis 3:1–6, which say that Satan taught "wisdom" and to know (to distinguish) between good and evil. This is the satanic confession of faith of Muhammad. He confirmed this oath in these verses.

Sura 2:50: "We gave Moses the book AND THE DISTINCTION, for guiding you by the right pathway." Distinction is synonymous with "distinguish."

Sura 3:2: "He has sent you the book, which confirms what was before it; he sent from above the Pentateuch and the Gospels to be guides for mankind. HE SENT THE "DISTINCTION.""

Sura 21:49: "We gave Moses and Aaron the distinction and the light and a clear warning for those who love the Lord."

Sura 25:1: "Blessed He who sent from above THE DIS-TINCTION (AL-FURQAN) TO HIS SERVANT, to make a warning to the mankind." The Sura (chapter) 25 has for name "Al-Furqan," which means "the distinction" (the distinction between good and evil); the usual explanations given by all Koran's translators of this word are misleading (or lies). This concept was so important for Muhammad that he decided to call a whole chapter with this name.

Sura 77:4: I swear "for those who establish the distinction." THE KORAN DOES NOT HAVE ANY IDEA, WORDS, FACTS, OR THEOPHANY THAT MAKE US THINK THAT THE WORD "DISTINCTION" HAS A DIFFERENT MEANING FROM THAT IN GENESIS CONCERNING THE DISTINCTION BETWEEN GOOD AND EVIL.

✿　　✿　　✿

Muhammad considered that David and Solomon were holy kings, worthy of dignity and respect. He considered they were saints who today are in the presence of God. He expressed these opinions in the following verses:

Sura 2:252: "They were put on flight with the authorization of God. David killed Djalut AND GOD GAVE HIM THE BOOK AND THE WISDOM." Djalut is probably Goliath. This is the first time the name of David appears in the Koran and Muhammad immediately starts saying that David had "wisdom."

Sura 4:161: "We gave the Psalms to David." This is repeated in 17:57.

Sura 6:84: "Among the descendants of Abraham we guided were also David and Solomon. . . . That's the way we reward those who make good."

Sura 21:78, 79 and 80: "Also remember David and Solomon when they pronounced a sentence concerning a farm where a flock caused some damage. . . . We gave Solomon the intelligence of this problem AND WE GAVE THEM BOTH THE POWER AND WISDOM. . . . We taught David the art of making shields."

Sura 27:15 and 16: "We gave the science to David and Solomon. They said: Praise the Lord who preferred us before many of his servants. Solomon was the heir of David. We have been taught the language of birds. . . . It is an evident favor from God."

Sura 34:12: the genii (demons) that work for Solomon "executed for him every works he wanted, palaces, statutes. . . . Oh family of David! . . . There are few grateful men among my servants." Sura 34:11 also speaks about this genii and Solomon. Satan is sometimes called Eblis in the Koran. Sura 18:48 says that Satan was one of the genii: "When we said to the angels: Prostrate before Adam, all did it, except Eblis, who was one of the genii; he rebelled against God."

Sura 38:16 through 25: "Endure with patience their words, Oh Muhammad! And remember our servant David, a powerful man, he used to come to us. We consolidated his empire. WE GAVE HIM THE WISDOM and the ability of dealing with your diferences," and also about David, the verse says, "WE FORGAVE HIM, WE GAVE HIM IN PARADISE A PLACE NEAR US AND A BEAUTIFUL HOUSE . . . Oh David . . . do not follow your passion, they take you away from the way of God." Muhammad is speaking there about the love of David for the wife of Urias, whom David killed to keep his wife. I already proved that God never forgave David.

Sura 38:29: "And we bestowed on David, Solomon. WHAT AN EXCELLENT SERVANT! He liked to turn toward God." These verses of the Koran depict David as a holy person.

The following verses present Solomon as another holy man.

Sura 2:95 and 96: "When the apostle went to them sent by God, confirming their holy books, one part of those who have received the scriptures put the book of God on their backs, pretending not to know it. They believed what the demons had thought about the power of Solomon; BUT SOLOMON WAS NOT THE UNFAITHFUL, but the demons."

Sura 4:161: "We gave you the revelation, as we gave it to Noah and the prophets. We gave it to Abraham . . . Job . . . Solomon, and we gave the Psalms to David." Muhammad considered Solomon as important as the prophets.

Sura 6:84: "Among the descendants of Abraham we also guided David and Solomon. . . . That's the way we reward those who do good," so according to Muhammad, Solomon was a good follower of God.

Sura 21:79 was already analyzed; it says, "We gave Solomon the intelligence of this matter and we gave them the power and wisdom." The true father of the Jewish-satanic tradition of "wisdom" is David; he is the first in the Bible who is ascribed as a believer of the satanic oath. But Solomon is the one who represents wisdom in the Bible because among other reasons, he wrote the Book of Wisdom. The satanism of Solomon in the Bible is more obvious than David's; the satanism of David is veiled, for this reason the satanic Jews chose David and not Solomon as their spiritual leader.

Sura 21:81 and 82: "We put the wind under the control of Solomon and we put under his control those demons who dive to search for pearls." The contradiction of Muhammad concerning Solomon is evident: on one side he said that Solomon was a holy person and on the other hand he said that Solomon was associated with demons.

Sura 27:15: "We gave the science to David and Solomon." The "science" is the science of the fruit of the tree of good and evil.

Sura 27:17: "One day the army of Solomon, composed of genii and men, stand before him. . . ." Sura 27:20 through 45 narrates the relation of Solomon with the Queen of Sheba, who "worships the Sun beside God." The Bible also speaks about the relation of Solomon with the Queen of Sheba. The Koran says that Solomon sent a letter to the Queen of Sheba with this salutation: "In the name of the merciful God, do not rise up against me, instead come to me, and turn entirely to God." Then the queen sent a messenger to Solomon and the king said to the messenger, "What God has given to me has more value than what he gave to you," and Solomon prepared his army to attack the queen and also asked the genii to volunteer in order to bring him the throne of the queen, and the "OTHER GENII, THE ONE WHO HAD THE SCIENCE OF THE BOOK, told Solomon: I will bring it to you before you blink"; later in the story, Solomon convinced the queen to obey God and not to worship idols, and the queen said, "Now I accept the will of God like Solomon does." This story showed the contradictory relation of Solomon with God and the genii (demons).

Sura 38:33 through 36: "We tested Solomon putting on his throne a shapeless body. Solomon, full of repentance, returned to us," asks for forgiveness, and he was forgiven but also "we put THE DEMONS, ALL OF THEM ARCHITECTS, under his control. . . . Also SOLOMON OCCUPIES A PLACE NEAR US AND ENJOYS THE MOST BEAUTIFUL HOUSE." Also the Freemasons associate Solomon with the idea of "architects," mainly because Solomon built the Temple of Jerusalem. So according to Muhammad, Solomon is in heaven with God.

Many people believe that the Koran has good opinions about Jesus Christ. Those people do not read the Koran and therefore ignore the real truth. Other people (including the book's authors) do read the Koran and even though they say that the Koran treats Jesus with dignity, they speak like false prophets, with lies. Muhammad denigrates Christ, as we can see in the following verses.

Sura 2:81: "We gave Moses the book of the law . . . we gave JESUS, SON OF MARY, evident signs. . . ." The point here is that Muhammad never said "Christ, the son of God" because he (as all the Judaists) did not believe that Jesus is the son of God. So Muhammad's opinion implies that Jesus is a liar because it was Christ himself who said that he is the son of God. In this verse Muhammad criticizes the Jews because they used to kill the prophets. This criticism is an expression of the ignorance of Muhammad about the Bible; he (being a Judaist) criticized the Jews because he did not have a deep knowledge of his own belief and group: Muhammad was illiterate; he did not know reading; he kept in his memory what some Jews taught him.

Sura 2:130: "We believe in the books that were given to Moses and Jesus." Here he mentions Christ without saying something of value.

Sura 4:155 and 156: "They haven't believed in Jesus; they have created against Mary a huge lie. They say: We condemned to death the Messiah, Jesus, son of Mary, the messenger of God. But they did not kill him, they did not crucify him, a man who looked like him was put on his place . . . they did not kill him for certain. God took him up unto himself." This is a terrible opinion of Muhammad against one of the holiest of the Christian theophany: the death and resurrection of Jesus Christ. Muhammad didn't believe that Christ was crucified.

Sura 4:169: "The Messiah, Jesus, son of Mary, is the apostle of God, and his Word, that he put on Mary, is a spirit who came from God," but Muhammad (being ignorant, illiterate, and blasphemous) adds, "Believe, then, in God and his apostles, and do not say: there is a trinity. Cease! . . . God is only one. Glory to him. HOW CAN HE HAVE A SON?" Here Muhammad does not believe in another basic Christian belief: the existence of the Trinity: the Father, the Son, and the Holy Spirit.

The following verses clearly establish that Muhammad is an antichrist. I already showed that he is a Davidian Satanist (a follower of David). The Davidian Satanists waited (and are still waiting) a Messiah descending from David. Christ broke this belief when coming to the world as the Messiah, the Son of God, who taught about peace and love. The Messiah the Jews are waiting for, is a human being full of political, religious, and military power, and also full of "wisdom," who will rule the world from Israel. Thus says Muhammad about Christ, the Messiah:

Sura 5:19: "THOSE WHO SAY THAT GOD IS THE MESSIAH, SON OF MARY, ARE UNBELIEVERS, AN-SWER THEM: WHO CAN AVOID THAT GOD COULD KILL THE MESSIAH, SON OF MARY, IF HE WISHES TO DO SO. . . ." The next Sura also says something similar.

Sura 5:76: "Unbeliever is the one who says: God is the Messiah, son of Mary. . . . To those who associate other gods to God, God will forbid him of the entrance to the garden, and his house will be the fire." So according to Muhammad, the Christians will go to the inferno, which is full of fire. Muhammad did not consider Jesus as the Messiah and son of God, but a simple messenger in the verse:

Sura 5:79: "The Messiah, son of Mary, WAS NONE OTHER THAN AN APOSTLE, HE WAS PRECEDED BY OTHER APOSTLES." Muhammad said that Jesus was a believer in the Satanic wisdom tradition:

Sura 5:110: about Jesus, "I taught you the book and the wisdom, the Pentateuch and the Gospel, you made with clay the figure of a bird with my authorization, you cured a blind and a leprous with my authorization . . . but the incredulous said: All these things are not other than magic." The making of a bird of clay by Jesus is an old Jewish fable that Muhammad knew and quoted; he presented Jesus as a magician, which is a lie. Christ believed in the Prophets, who rejected magic and astrology.

Sura 5:116: "Then God said to Jesus: HAVE YOU SAID TO MANKIND: TAKE AS GODS MY MOTHER AND ME? . . . HOW COULD I HAVE SAID WHAT IS NOT TRUE."

Sura 6:89: says that to "Jesus" and others, "we gave them the Scriptures, THE WISDOM AND THE PROPHECIES," we already know that Jesus only believed in the "Law and the Prophets" and rejected the wisdom. Sura 2:79 says, "WOULD YOU BELIEVE IN ONE PART OF YOUR BOOK AND REJECT ANOTHER? WHAT WILL BE THE REWARD FOR THOSE WHO DO THAT? THE IGNOMINY IN THIS WORLD, AND THE DAY OF THE RESURRECTION THEY WILL RECEIVE THE MOST CRUEL PUNISHMENT." Muhammad is speaking there about Jesus, so he knew that Christ rejected the wisdom and even though he said that God gave Jesus the wisdom, he is not speaking about the Jews who rejected the Gospel, because as I proved, Muhammad is a follower of Judaism and the Davidian satanism.

Sura 9:30: "The Jews say: Ozair is the son of God. The Christians say: the Messiah is the son of God. These are the words from their mouths, and by saying this they are like the unbelievers of other times. May God make war against them! They are liars." The idea that the Jews considered Ozair as son of God is not in the Bible; this is another proof that Muhammad learned from other books (non-biblical books) of the Judaism.

Sura 9:31: "They have taken wise men and monks and the Messiah, the son of Mary, as their masters (instead of God). . . . Far from his glory the divinities they associate to God!"

Sura 19:31: "I am the servant of God, Jesus told them; he gave me the book and made me a prophet." Muhammad does not believe that Jesus is the Messiah, but just a simple prophet, this idea came from the Judaists, those who killed Christ.

Sura 19:35 and 36: "Jesus, son of Mary, spoke the truth," but the ignorant, confused, and illiterate Muhammad said (in verse 36) "God cannot have a son. Far from his glory this blasphemy."

Sura 43:59: "Jesus is no other than a servant . . . who is an example for the son of Israel."

Sura 43:63: "When Jesus came to mankind . . . he said: I bring the WISDOM to you and come to explain the object of our dispute."

Sura 57:27: "We sent after them other apostles, like Jesus, son of Mary." The next verse contains another lie of Muhammad; he quoted Jesus, but what he quoted is not in any book in the world:

Sura 61:6: "Jesus, son of Mary, said to his people: Oh son of Israel! I am the apostle of God, I was sent to you to confirm the Pentateuch that was given to you before me. I WAS ALSO SENT TO ANNOUNCE YOU THE COMING OF AN APOSTLE AFTER ME, WHOSE NAME WILL BE AHMED," which means Muhammad. Christ said that the last prophet was John the Baptist (Matthew 11:13) and he never said that another prophet would come after him. Note to the reader: the contradiction and confusion in the mind of Muhammad: sometimes he denigrates Christ, but here Jesus plays the role of announcing the coming of Muhammad. Others verses that speak subtly about Christ are:

Sura 5:16, 17, and 18: "They twist the words of the Scriptures and forget a part of what was taught to them. . . . We also accepted the covenant of those who say: we are Christians, but they forgot a part of what was taught to them. . . . Oh you who have received the Scripture! Our messenger has indicated to you many verses you kept in secret." He clearly speaks there about the Christians, who rejected the Book of Wisdom.

Sura 18:3 and 4: the Koran is "a book destined to warn those who say: God has a son . . . is a great sin this words they say. IT IS A LIE."

Other verses that say something similar are: 2:110, 2:256, 3:73, 6:51, 100 and 101, 10:3 and 69, 19:36, 19:92 and 93, 21:26, 23:93, 25:2, 37:152 through 156, 39:6, 43:14, 17, 81 and 82, and the 72:3.

Throughout this book I have mentioned many of the characteristics of the satanists: pyramids, human sacrifices, astrology, the belief in the doctrine of wisdom, the anti-Christianism, etc. (Another way of identifying Satanists is: by their symbolism, their own confession of satanic faith, and/or by the murder(s) they commit). I have mentioned in this chapter the ideas of Muhammad that describe him as a Satanist. The following verses contain more ideas that support my point:

Sura 2:123: "Raise among them a messenger taken from them who will read the story of miracles and TEACH THEM THE BOOK AND THE WISDOM."

Sura 2:146: ". . . we sent you an apostle . . . who will read our teachings . . . and will teach you the book AND THE WISDOM." The "apostle" is Muhammad.

Sura 2:231: ". . . remember the benefits of God, of the book AND THE WISDOM HE SENT TO YOU FROM ABOVE."

Sura 2:272: God "gives the WISDOM to whom he wishes, and those who have obtained the WISDOM have obtained a great good thing."

Sura 3:73: "Is it convenient that the man to whom God gave the BOOK, THE WISDOM AND THE PROPHECY says to mankind: Be my worshipers." Here Muhammad insists that God gave Jesus "the Law, the wisdom and the Prophets," once again I have to say that Jesus only believed in "the Law and the Prophets" and rejected the Book of Wisdom because they contained the teachings of Satan, David, Solomon, and others.

Sura 3:75: "When God received the covenant of the prophets, he said: HERE IS THE BOOK AND THE WISDOM THAT I GIVE TO YOU." Other verses in which Muhammad defends the "wisdom" are: 3:158, 4:57 and 113, 12:22 (this says "we gave the wisdom and the science to Joseph"), 17:41, 19:13, 21:74, 31:11, 33:34 ("review . . . the teachings of the wisdom"), and the 43:1, 2 and 3 ("the Koran is full of wisdom"). Therefore the concept of Wisdom is of basic importance for Muhammad; that's why he speaks abundantly about it. The satanism of Muhammad is also expressed in:

Sura 15:16: "We established the signs of the ZODIAC in the sky, and we put them in order for those who watch." The Sura 2:181 says that the Koran was given from God to Muhammad during the "moon of Ramadan" (the month of Ramadan), which is an association of astronomy with religion; this is, by definition, astrology. The moon and a star are part of the symbolism of the Islamic religion (it can be seen in flags, for example). Sura 2:185 says, "They ask you about the new moon. Tell them: they are the time prepared to be useful for mankind AND TO INDICATE THE TIME OF THE PILGRIMAGE TO MECCA." The true prophets of the Bible criticized the worship of the new moon; the pagans used to commit human sacrifices on the day of the new moon and every day astronomical phenomena were observed in the sky. Sura 25:62: "BLESSED IS HIM WHO PUT IN THE SKY THE SIGN OF THE ZODIAC, who put the torch and the moon which give light." Sura 85:1: "I swear for the sky adorned with THE TWELVE SIGNS OF THE ZODIAC." Astrology was one of the main characteristics of the ancient people who practiced human sacrifices.

The Temple of Jerusalem was built by Solomon, the satanic beast 666, with the cooperation of the famous (also satanic) Phoenicians. Muhammad adored this temple and considered it a holy sanctuary. He said that in verse 17:1 "Glory to him who

146

transported his servant during the night from the holy temple of Mecca to the temple of Jerusalem, WHICH WE BLESSED, to show them our miracle."

The following verses are not necessarily related to Satanism, but I have to mention them because they speak about very important social and human problems. In these verses, Muhammad displays once more his evilish mentality.

Sura 2:228: "Men are first before women."

Sura 4:38: "MEN ARE SUPERIOR TO WOMEN, as a consequence of the qualities that God gave to men, which allow them to be above women . . . the good women are obedient, submissive . . . those you think are disobedient . . . scourge them." The women in Islamic countries live as second-class citizens, as slaves of men in power. The women of Islamic countries will never see liberation if they don't change their religion; the only option is to follow the entity who forgave that prostitute, the man who came to earth from heaven to cut the chain that Satan put on their necks: Jesus Christ. Women must be obedient and submissive, according to these other verses: 2:223, 4:128, 24:31, and 66:5.

Sura 2:187, about the worshipers of idols, "KILL THEM wherever you find them. . . . The temptation of idolatry is worse than the CARNAGE IN THE WAR." Sura 33:60 and 61 say, "We will incite you against them and you will exterminate them" and "Cursed they are in any place, they will be caught and KILLED IN THE MIDDLE OF A TERRIBLE CARNAGE." Sura 47:4: "When you find unbelievers, KILL THEM TO THE POINT OF MAKING A CARNAGE." In 1993 a group of terrorist Muslims put a truck full of explosives into the basement of one of the buildings of the World Trade Center in New York. They caused a tremendous explosion, with the intention of killing thousands of innocent elderly, women, children, and others, but they didn't succeed, and they only killed six persons.

This is the criminal attitude of those who follow the Koran, in obedience to the verses I mentioned above.

Millions of Muslims believe that this is a personal and wrong attitude of a few terrorist Muslim men, those millions don't read the Koran; they should read it in order to discover the truth about the Koran and Muhammad. According to the tradition (it is not written in the Koran) Muhammad ordered to kill one of his political opponents and the order was carried out.

Sura 5:34: "Cain was of those who repented," only an ignorant Satanist can pronounce this opinion. The Bible never says that Cain repented after killing Abel.

There are many data that link Muhammad with David. Muhammad was a Davidian satanist. The Koran contains many verses defending David. I have said that Islamism was not a new religion different from Judaism; actually the Koran IS A COMMENTARY ON THE BIBLE.

There is another connection between David and Muhammad, which has been kept in secret for fourteen centuries. Many Suras (chapters) have IN THE FIRST VERSE a few words that have no apparent meaning. Scholars say that they are "mysterious" words without a known significance. The following are all these words (and all chapters), which meaning is unknown:

Sura 2-1: "ALIF. LAM. MIM."
Sura 3-1: "ALIF. LAM. MIM."
Sura 7-1: "ALIF. LAM. MIN. SAD."
Sura 10-1: "ALIF. LAM. RA."
Sura 11-1: "ALIF. LAM. RA."
Sura 12-1: "ALIF. LAM. RA."
Sura 13-1: "ALIF. LAM. MIM. RA."
Sura 14-1: "ALIF. LAM. RA."
Sura 15-1: "ALIF. LAM. RA."
Sura 19-1: "KAF. HA. YA. AIN. SAD."

148

Sura 20-1: "TA. HA." (Also the name of the chapter is "TA. HA.")

Sura 26-1: "TA. SIN. MIM."

Sura 27-1: "TA. SAD."

Sura 28-1: "TA. SIN. MIM."

Sura 29-1: "ALIF. LAM. MIN."

Sura 30-1: "ALIF. LAM. MIM."

Sura 31-1: "ALIF. LAM. MIM."

Sura 32-1: "ALIF. LAM. MIM."

Sura 36-1: "YA. SIN." (It is also the name of the chapter.)

Sura 38-1: "SAD." (It is also the name of the chapter.)

Sura 40-1: "HA. MIM."

Sura 41-1: "HA. MIM."

Sura 42-1: "HA. MIM. AIN. SIN. QAF."

Sura 43-1: "HA. MIM."

Sura 44-1: "HA. MIM."

Sura 45-1: "HA. MIM."

Sura 46-1: "HA. MIM."

Sura 50-1: "QAF" (It is also the name of the chapter.)

Sura 68-1: "NUN."

This is a summary of all the letters: ALIF, LAM, MIM, SAD, RA, QAF, HA, YA, AIN, TA, SIN, and NUN. These are all the Suras of the Koran, which mentions these letters. The origin of these letters is the following: They are the characters of the Hebrew alphabet, which means they are the letters of the Hebrew alphabet. Muhammad was a Davidian follower who had inspiration from the Davidian Psalms and copied from them, not only these letters but also the writing style of the Koran, which is written in poetic verses like the Psalms of David. The imitation of David by Muhammad is complete, not only in the theological aspect, but also in the literary aspect. Because Muhammad wrote the Koran in poetic verses, he was called by some of his contemporaries "a poet." For example, the Koran 52:30 says, "They will say: he is a poet," and in 69:41 "God" says, "It is not the word of a poet."

The following are the Psalms of David that contain the characters of the Hebrew alphabet. They are mentioned AT THE BEGINNING of verses:

Psalm 34 verse 1: "Psalms of David, when he feigned madness before Abimelech, so that he drove him out, and he could escape."

verse	verse	verse
2: ALEPH	9: TETH	16: AIN
3: BETH	10: YOD	17: PE
4: GHIMEL	11: KAPH	18: SADE
5: DALETH	12: LAMED	19: QOPH
6: HE	13: MEM	20: RESH
7: ZAIN	14: NUN	21: SHIN
8: HETH	15: SAMEK	22: TAU

The letters VAU appear in other Psalms. The other Psalms that contain all or many of these letters are: 9, 10, 25, 37, 111, 112, 119, and 145. Psalms 10, 111, 112, and 119 do not say that they are of David; the rest say that they are Psalms of David. The "PH" at the end of some words is also written as "f." I will use the "f" in the next explanation.

The concordance between the Psalms of David and the verses of the Koran:

Psalms of David:	Verses of the Koran:
Alef	Alif
Lamed	Lam
Mem	Mim
Sade	Sad
Resh	Ra
Kaf	Qaf
He	Ha
Yod	Ya
Ain	Ain
Tau	Ta
Shin	Sin
Nun	Nun

Muhammad did not include in the Koran the other letters that are in David's Psalms, and the letters he included in the Koran are not in order. The reason for this is that Muhammad most probably did not have the Hebrew Scriptures when he was dictating the Koran to his secretary; Muhammad didn't know reading and writing. What he dictated to his secretary was in his memory, and for this reason, he forgot the other letters. These Hebrew characters are also in the biblical book of Proverbs 31:10–31, which is a book belonging to the satanic wisdom tradition and attributed to Solomon. They also appear in the biblical book of "Lamentations," chapters 1, 2, 3 and 4. This book is attributed to Jeremiah, the prophet. But Jeremiah is not the author of this book because this book is blasphemous; its content is similar to many of the satanic David's Psalms. These words are only used in the Bible by Satanists and also in the Koran; they are not found in any other sacred book of any religion.

18. The "Wisdom," A Driving Force of the Satanists

We have seen that the Satanists have elaborated a theory based on "wisdom." "Wisdom" means to the Satanists, among other things, to have a complete knowledge about religion, politics, the economy, sciences, etc., and to use these knowledges for getting "power." "Power" means to have the capacity to produce and accumulate goods and monetary power, which can be used to be the master of peoples and nations. To get this power, "the end justified the way," so if they have to kill or plan and carry out war and genocides, they do it. And they have been doing this for about fifty centuries. For this reason the Judaists and others Satanists dream of being the "masters of the universe," and for this reason, they have been infiltrating successfully all the nations and all groups with power.

The followers of God knew the existence of this satanic wisdom. Isaiah 5:21 says "Woe unto them who are wise before their own eyes." Isaiah 28:9, making ridicule of pagans, says: "whom he will teach wisdom?" and in 29:14 it says "I will do again amazing things with this people. THE SCIENCE OF THE WISE COULD DO NOTHING AGAINST THEM." In 29:24 the prophet says "THOSE WITH BAD SOUL WILL LEARN THE WISDOM." Jeremiah 8:8 and 9 say, "How do you say: We have the wisdom, we possess the Law of Yahweh?" James (Jesus' brother, according to some) says in 3:15 speaking about the wisdom of the pagans: "SUCH WISDOM DOES NOT COME DOWN FROM ABOVE, IT IS AN EARTHLY,

ANIMAL, DEMONIC WISDOM." About the satanic wisdom and its followers, Jesus said to his "generation" who disobey God: "AND THE WISDOM IS JUSTIFIED BY HIS DEEDS," which are the deeds of the satanic Judaists including the Pharisees (read Matthew 11:19).

The belief of Satan (to distinguish between good and evil) according to Genesis 3:1–6, was known by the prophets; therefore they never used this expression because they knew the meaning of it.

Another satanic book in the Bible is Ecclesiasticus (part of the Books of Wisdom, called "Sirach" in some Bibles). This book also contains the satanic confession of faith as written in 17:6 and 24:33–36: the Lord to the men "filled them WITH SCIENCE AND UNDERSTANDING AND TAUGHT THEM TO KNOW GOOD AND EVIL," and the Law is said to be "FULL OF WISDOM LIKE THE PISHON WITH WATER, LIKE THE TIGRIS IN THE SEASON OF FRUIT; FULL OF UNDERSTANDING LIKE THE EUPHRATES IS FULL OF WATER," it is clearly talking about the paradise (the Garden of Eden) of Genesis 2:11–14 and 3:1–6, which mentioned those three rivers where Satan taught wisdom and also to know good from evil (which is the same as saying "good AND evil").

I have to mention here once more that the biblical Book of Wisdom is in reality two books in one; one is satanic, the other is not. Chapters 1 through 10 are satanic, but chapters 11 through 19 are not satanic; precisely in the last book, the wisdom is condemned.

Satan on Modern Time. Continuation

In previous chapters I explained the satanism of David and Solomon, who are the spiritual fathers of the men who govern

Europe, America, and almost all the nations of the world. I have said that the Freemasons are the most powerful followers of Lucifer (Lucifer means: the one who brings the light, the wisdom; from the Latin *lux,* light, and *ferre,* to bring). The Freemasons said that they are the heirs of all the wisdom of the ancient people; this is true. The Masons have as a basic story and "mystery" the construction of the Temple of Solomon, and they considered this king as one of their spiritual fathers.

Those who can read books written by Masons easily realize that the phraseology and concepts of the Masons are: 1) pagan, and also 2) Judaic, and based on the beliefs of the Jewish Satanists who believe in the "wisdom" tradition. The Masons extract most of their religious concepts from the Bible, and the most fundamental beliefs are inspired in the beast 666 and also in those Jews called "rebels" in the Bible. (Isaiah 48:8 said of the Judaists: "Your name is Rebel since the day you were born.")

The legend of Hiram is one of the fundamentals of Freemasonry. The Bible speaks about Hiram, king of Tyre, a Phoenician city, who helped Solomon to build the temple. In the Masonic story, the descendants of the murderer Cain have a positive main role (in the person of Tubal Cain); Solomon plays the main role. The story is about a fictitious event that happened during the construction of the Temple of Solomon. The real intention of the story is to expose with "a veil" their real belief in Solomon and his satanism, but many non-Masons cannot take out the veil and see the reality (as do many Masons). All the ancient nations committed human sacrifices during the celebration of "mysteries," the Masons have also made human sacrifices, as I will explain.

*   *   *

A subliminal message is one that is sent to a person through his eye or ears, but the person who receives the message does not realize that he is receiving a message. There are subliminal satanic messages everywhere in allmost every city in the world.

The USA bills have subliminal messages. In the one dollar bill, at the left of the circle (with a drawn pyramid), there is a tail of a rattlesnake. In ancient times wherever there were pyramids, also existed (drawn or carved) a serpent in the same pyramids or in temples. For this reason there is a pyramid and a serpent drawn in this bill. Alongside a white line (on the side of the bill where the pyramid is), which is the limit between the central area and the peripheral area that looks like the skin of a serpent, there are many figures of small serpents (for example, exactly above and near the words "IN GOD WE TRUST"). Two tails of a serpent can also be seen on the right side of the circle with the pyramid. Tails of serpents can also be see on both sides of the circle with the eagle.

Inside the circle with the pyramid, there are these words: "Annuit Coeptis, Novus Ordo Seclorum," which mean "we announce the birth of a new secular order." Secular means: not related to religion or church; there is a secret message that simply means that they are not Christians (the Masons). The serpents mean that they believe in the Serpent, Satan. The pyramid is not part of the symbolism of the Christians. Its presence there means that they believe in the religion that built pyramids. At the bottom of the pyramid, on the right side, there is a cactus, which is a tree that only was found in America in pre-Columbian time. Therefore the pyramid of the dollar bill is not an Egyptian pyramid (as some Masons claim), but an American pyramid in which millions of humans were killed to honor the Serpent (for example, Quetzalcoatl in Mexico and Kukulkan in Mayan lands; both names mean plumed serpent). Masons claim that the Egyptians didn't make human sacrifices, which is an obvious lie, so they say that the pyramid on the dollar has no relation with human sacrifices, which is another lie (because it is an American pyramid). Flavius Josephus clearly said that the Egyptians did make human sacrifices. And the figure of the Pharaoh "smiting the enemies" (the Pharaoh holding enemies by their hairs and having a knife in the right hand) is a representation of the human sacrifices committed by Pharaohs.

The words "IN GOD WE TRUST" do not refer to the God of Abraham and the Christians, but to Satan who is the god-architect of pyramids and is represented by a serpent. So in 1776, with the birth of the USA, was also born a new order that had as a master the god of pyramids, the Serpent. The eye above the pyramid is the eye of Horus (an Egyptian god; by this reason many believe that this is an Egyptian pyramid). Horus used to be represented by a falcon. The eye of Horus in the bill is surrounded by sun rays, which are a representation of one of the most important gods in Egypt: the sun-god. Above the eagle that is in the circle, there are thirteen stars, they are arranged forming a star of David, the main symbol of Judaism. The Jews created Freemasonry and draw the star of David as a subliminal message, which is a usual practice of the Masons and all the Satanists. (I have to repeat here that few followers of Judaism are Satanists; most of them are good and valuable persons, but THEY IGNORE THE REALITY BEHIND THEIR BELIEFS.) On the other side of the one dollar bill, there is a square, a Masonic symbol. There is also on this side a drawing of George Washington, a Mason, the "liberator" of the U.S.A., and its first president.

The five-dollar bill has an oval, with two branches on both sides. This is a subliminal manner of drawing the main Egyptian gods: the serpent and the sun-god. The oval and the two branches represent the winged solar disk. An oval or a circle with two branches on both sides is one of the most frequently used symbols of the Masons. Remember that the winged solar disk was used by all the pagan civilizations in the ancient world; the circle represents the sun-god and the branches represent the wings of the plumed serpent; the winged solar disk usually had two serpents on both sides of the circle. This symbol was mixed with the Jews' symbol of the two branches of olive and the lampstand in the center. This last Jewish symbol was born from the vision of the Jewish prophet Zechariah, which says in his biblical book in chapter 4 verses 2 and 3, "I see a lampstand, made of gold, with a bowl on top of it and with seven lamps, with seven lips from the lamps to the bowl that is above; and by it there are two olive branches, one at the right of the bowl and the other to the left." We can see this symbol in the shield of modern Israel.

Another subliminal symbol used frequently by Masons is an undulant band, sometimes accompanied by two branches, sometimes by a circle. This undulant band is a subliminal, semi-secret manner of representing a serpent. The two branches represent here the wings of a bird, every leaf represents a feather, so the undulant band with the two branches represents here the Plumed Serpent. Like the ancient Egyptians, the Free-masons used to modify symbols. In ancient civilations, the serpent-god was represented either by plumes or without them. The oval and the undulant band with two branches can be seen at the top of the main door in many buildings in America and Europe.

The ten dollar bill has two big "S"s around the number 10, which is in every corner. The "S" is the first letter of the names Satan, Solomon, and Serpent. There are also many small figure of serpents. On the other side of this bill, there is in the center and between the two superior corners the head of a cobra; the cobra was the symbol of the Egyptian royalty and the Pharaohs had an image of it in the forehead.

The twenty-dollar bill has a drawing of Andrew Jackson, one of the first presidents; his left hand is near the central area of the chest; it is an imitation of the same posture adopted by the Pharaohs (usually the right hand). This same posture is typical of Washington, Napoleon, and other famous Masons.

George Washington was a Mason and president of the Society of Cincinnati, Lodge 22. There were many Masons as leaders of the USA independence. Eight of those who signed the Declaration of Independence were Masons: Benjamin Franklin, John Hancock, Joseph Herwes, William Hooper, Robert Payne, Richard Stockton, George Walton, and William Whipley. It is said that seventeen of all the North American presidents have been Masons. Most probably they all were members of secret "fraternities," secret satanic societies. All the "liberators" ("fathers of the countries") of Latin American countries were Masons, including Simon Bolivar, Jose Marti (Cuba), and Juan Pablo Duarte (in the Dominican Republic). Kings, princes, emperors, generals, and other men in power were Masons (in the past).

Today the world is very corrupt and very close to reviving the Serpent's Empire: satanic "churches," offices of spiritists, witchcraft, astrologists, gnostics. Also abortion, homosexuality, lesbianism, drug addiction, murders and assaults every minute, parents who rape their children, satanic music, gay marriages, etc. Today there is a widespread proliferation of all kinds of perverts and evildoers. This is the direct result of a world governed by the satanic Freemasons who have the secret help and connivance of the highest authorities of the Vatican and other institutions. The Satanists have made popular in USA the celebration of Halloween, an ancient feast celebrated by the Druids, the priests of the Celts, worshipers of the sun-god (in the north of Europe, especially in England), during which human sacrifices were carried out. Today during this feast, millions of children wear monstrous masks and many adults do evil things like burning abandoned houses and giving as a gift poisoned candies.

Leviticus 18:22 (a Bible book) says concerning homosexuality: "You shall not lie with man like with a woman, it is an abomination"; today a good number of Protestant pastors say that homosexuality is a right thing to do. This practice has increased the number of patients with perianal fistules (due to a virus called Herpes simplex), gonorrhea, syphilis, AIDS, and other diseases.

The activity of the Masons in France have been important in the past. Napoleon was most probably a Mason and a Jacobin. It is known that he protected the Freemasonry. He went to Egypt to conquer that land but also to rescue from oblivion the temples, pyramids, and documents of the ancients. One of the French soldiers discovered the "Rosetta stone," which has an inscription in Greek, hieroglyphic, and demotic (the common ancient Egyptian people's language); this discovery allowed a better study and understanding of the Egyptian ancient civilization.

During the French Revolution (carried out by the Masons), anti-Christianism was the rule. The revolutionaries created a new religion named Theophilanthropy or the Religion of Reason, a subliminal name given to the religion of wisdom. Many of the revolutionaries were clearly Masons; others preferred to keep in secret their memberships. The same thing happened during the USA War of Independence, the Soviet Revolution, and the independence of the Latin American countries; the same thing is happening today. Many members deny that they are Masons.

Among the prominent Masonic personalities of the French Revolution were: Lafayette (a general who years before had helped the North American revolutionaries), Marat, Robespierre, Danton, and Voltaire (this last one was one of the famous Encyclopedists who helped to create the philosophical and political fundamentals of the Revolution; he died years before the revolution started). The French revolutionaries produced the document called "The Universal Declaration of Human Rights," but a few years later, they took off the masks and showed the world their true satanic identity: they established "the Reign of Terror," a dictatorship during which they created the guillotine in order to decapitate the supposed enemies. (Hitler also used the guillotine.) The decapitation was an imitation of the Pharaohs smiting the enemies: the Egyptian kings decapitated prisoners as offerings to some gods. After the "Reign of Terror" came the dictatorship of Napoleon and the European Napoleonic wars, which tainted the continent red by the bloodshed.

In Mexico there was a movement called "the Reform" in the last century (the nineteenth century). It caused important and permanent changes in the socio-politics of Mexico. The leader was Benito Juarez, a Mason. The "Reform" was also an anti-Christian movement; its effects persist today. The flag and shield of Mexico have a drawing of an eagle with a serpent in its mouth; it is a subliminal message, which means that the men in power in Mexico believe in the Plumed Serpent, Satan. The North American Masons were timid and didn't dare to draw a serpent with an eagle; instead they drew an undulant band in the mouth of the eagle, as we can see in the one dollar bill. The band represents the serpent.

Many countries have in their flags and shields symbols created by the Masons. The projection of the Masons is worldwide: they want to be the master of the world. These are some of the countries that use Masonic symbols in their flags or shields:

Argentina: two branches (one on the right and the other to the left, inspired by Zechariah, the biblical prophet), the Phrygian cap (ancient symbol of Mitras, the Sun-god, and one of the main symbols of the French Revolution), the Masonic handshaking, the fasces (ancient Roman symbol, which means authority).
Bolivia: two branches, Phrygian cap.

Bahamas: Phrygian cap, sun (the sun-god), undulant band (the serpent).

Brazil: two branches, sun, band.

Bulgaria: two branches.

Canada: two branches, band.

Colombia: Phrygian cap, band, bird with a serpent in the mouth, the god of fortune.

Costa Rica: two branches, band, sun.

Cuba: Phrygian cap, two branches, sun, fasces.

Chipre: two branches.

Dominican Republic: two branches, band (the first flag included a serpent, a Phrygian cap, and cannon balls in a pyramidal form).

Ecuador: two branches, sun, bird, fasces.

Salvador: band, Phrygian caps, pyramid.

Spain: bird and band (the plumed serpent), two columns (the two famous columns of the Temple of Solomon).

USA: bird with a band in the mouth, two branches.

France: two branches, band.

Haiti: Phrygian cap, two crossed cannons (imitating the crossed arms of the Pharaoh), and cannon balls in a pyramidal form.

Honduras: pyramid, sun, two columns.

Nicaragua: pyramid, sun, Phrygian cap.

Peru: two branches, the fortune god.

Pakistan: two branches, band.

East Germany: compass, band.

Venezuela: two branches, band, the fortune god.

Hungary: two branches.

Israel: TWO BRANCHES.

Italy: two branches, band.

Syria: bird, band, two branches.

Russia: two branches, and crossed sickle and hammer.

The United Nations organization (U.N.) uses as a main symbol the circle (the sun-god) and two branches on both sides of the circle. The U.N. is the foreign relations office of the Freemasons and other Satanists who control the world.

The independence of The Dominican Republic was carried out by a secret organization named "the Trinitary" (from the biblical Trinity). Its members used secret signs for communication (as the Masons). Many of its leaders were Masons. The main leader, Juan Pablo Duarte, was a member of the lodge "Constante Union" (Constant Union) No. 8 in Santo Domingo. The day they created this secret society, they signed the oath with blood drawn from some of their fingers in violation of Bible advice.

From 1930 to 1961, the Dominican Republic was governed by a demonic and a murderous beast named Rafael Leonidas Trujillo. He killed 12,000 humans (children, elderly, and young) in one week because they were not white like him and because they were foreigners living in the country (they were Haitians). During his thirty-one years reign this dictator killed thousands of political adversaries and freedom fighters. One night in 1961, on a dark solitary road, he was chased and killed by his own friends. This dictator was a Mason.

This Dominican criminal dictator had a minister who was a lawyer and diplomatic and probably the main "brain" of his government for those thirty-one years of terror. He was his right hand. His name is Joaquin Balaguer. In 1992 the president of the country (Joaquin Balaguer) inaugurated, with the presence of the pope, the first pyramid built in America after the year 1492. The name of this pyramid is "the Columbus Lighthouse," and it is, supposedly, a monument to honor Columbus and the Christianism he brought to America. The monument was designed by an English architect (J. L. Gleave), taking inspiration from the Amerindian pyramids, as he said himself. He said that its silhouette reminded him of the Egyptian Sphinx and AN

AZTEC SERPENT. The building is a modified pyramid. Inside there are the remains of Columbus. The ancient Amerindian rulers, "el Senor de Palenque" and "el Senor de Sipan," were also buried in pyramids. Some Egyptian pyramids were prepared as tombs. At the main entrance of the Santo Domingo Pyramid, there is a plaque dedicated to the workers who died during its construction; the plaque says that the builders appreciate "the sacrifice" done by those who offered their lives during the construction. The word "sacrifice" used in this context is a subliminal manner of talking about the human sacrifices done in pyramids. One of the external walls of this pyramid says (subliminally) that in ancient times America was visited by the pyramid builders. The obelisk of Santo Domingo, which is in the avenue known as "Malecon," was painted at the top with images of the sun (the Sun-God). The painting was permitted by men in power in the government; the party that was in power, (and allowed the painting) was created by Juan Bosch, a Mason. (The Dominican pyramid, Columbus lighthouse is depicted on the cover of this book with radiating light.)

Another frequently used Masonic symbol is two long objects (cannons, swords, rifles, etc.) crossed in the center, forming an "X." It can be seen in flags and shields. It is an imitation of the crossed arms of the Pharaohs; the meaning of the crossed arms is "power." In the uniforms of almost all the officers of the armies of almost every country, we can see in the neck or over the shoulders crossed swords or sticks. We can see that also in the uniforms of the Nazis.

19. Satan and His Human Sacrifices of the Twentieth Century

Six million innocent and naive (non-Satanist) Jews were killed from 1940–1945 in Europe. They were killed by Hitler and the Nazis. They were victims of the criminal and evil game played by their fellow Judaists and other Satanists who govern the nations who planned and fought in WWII, including Germany, England, Russia, and the United States. The satanist rulers of the time were Hitler, Stalin, Truman, and others. The 6 million Jews who were killed were believers in the God of Abraham. They were killed by a man who during his youth was a member of a secret satanic society in Germany (Adolf Hitler). Hitler sacrificed them to honor the devil. It is well known that many prominent members of Nazism were members of the secret society called Thule, in Germany. The Nazis worshiped the sun god, kept the obelisks that were already built in Germany, and planned to build more. One of the main symbols of the Nazis was the Iron Cross, which was the same cross used by the satanic Knights Templars. After 1945 it was said that Hitler had Jewish blood; so the reason he killed so many Jews was that he most probably was a satanic Jew and the victims were non-satanic Jews. The Reichstag (the main government building), designed by Albert Speer, had in the main salon images of the two branches, a Jewish satanic symbol. The satanic Nazism was inspired by the ideas of Friedrich Nietzsche (A.D. 1844–1900). Nietzsche said in his book, *Thus Spake Zarathustra,* that he is a follower of Satan. He said that the eagle and the serpent are the entities he loves. He loves: the flying eagle with a serpent, and a "wise serpent" around a "golden sun." He also said that one day will come a "superdragon." He also said in the same book that he loves together: the sun, the eagle, and the serpent. All of these concepts clearly refer to the plumed serpent (Satan) and his variation, the winged solar disc. In a poem within *Thus Spake Zarathustra,* Neitzsche uses the word "Selah." He didn't explain the meaning of this word. This word can also be read in some Davidian and non-Davidian Psalms in which the word doesn't have a clear meaning either. The use of this word is a kind of secret message. Nietzsche also wrote *The Antichrist,* in which he confesses that he is a satanist.

At the end of WWII, the president of U.S.A. was Harry Truman. He was a well-known Freemason. He committed the most horrendous genocide and the biggest human sacrifice ever done by a beast: on August 6 and 9 of 1945, he dropped over Hiroshima and Nagasaki in Japan two atomic bombs killing immediately more than 150,000 human beings, including children, elderly, and young; the victims were very far away from battlefields. The sacrificers gave the public ridiculous excuses that even today the North American people do not believe.

In Russia, for about thirty years, the ruler was Joseph Stalin, a dictator of Communist Russia. He killed about 20 million people, his own people. The Soviet Revolution was made by the same followers of the religion of pyramids and human sacrifices, the same people who also made the French and North American revolutions, and the independence of Latin American countries. Five of the highest leaders of the Soviet Revolution and later ministers of the Communist government were Masons: Kerensky, Tereshchenko, Nekrasov, Konovalov, and Lvov. And because the leaders of the revolution believed in the religion of pyramids, they buried Lenin in a pyramid called "the Lenin Mausoleum;" it is a pyramid very similar to those pyramids in Egypt and America. Many say that Lenin had Jewish blood. Trotsky, another prominent leader, also had Jewish blood. Many believe that Karl Marx was member of a secret satanic society; his theory about the struggle of the opposites was inspired in the "dualism" of Satan's oath (to know good and evil), a subliminal way of believing in the concept of knowing good and evil (opposite forces). Marx's belief in "Dialectic" was inspired by Aristotle's *Topics*. This book deals with a technique to analize the "opposites," including the "knowledge of good and evil." Karl Marx was Jewish.

The maximum leader of the plan that destroyed communism in Russia was Mikhail Gorbachev; in order to carry out his plan, he was helped by the pope and by ex-president Ronald Reagan. In a newspaper article that I read in Santo Domingo in 1992, Gorbachev said: that he would continue with Perestroika and Glasnost without paying attention to those who warned him about the "Jewish-Masonic" conspiracy. But we should ask: is not Gorbachev member of that group?

The men in power in U.S.A. had about eight decades of telling the world that they were enemy of the Soviet Union. They never fought directly on a battlefield. Many died in Korea and Vietnam, thinking that they were fighting against an enemy, the Communists. About 58,000 died in Vietnam fighting against Communists. Thousands died in Latin America fighting in order to create Communist states. The money to buy machine guns and bullets came in part from the Soviet Union. But the White House never was an enemy of the red Kremlin. They both were created by Masons. For this reason the USA cooperated with the Soviet Union in its war against the Nazis; and when the war was over, some men in power in the USA told the Soviets the secrets of building atomic bombs, instead of sending them an ultimatum saying: you planned to destroy USA, now we have atomic bombs, so either you dismantle communism or face total annihilation. But there is a basic rule inside Freemasonry: a brother should not betray a brother, especially should not kill him.

Temples of ancient Egypt have the typical posture of the Pharaohs smiting (sacrificing) the enemies to honor some gods. The same posture is seen in Amerindian rulers. The Pharaoh Amenhotep II wrote on a wall of a temple in Karnak that he sacrificed some enemies. The Pharaohs and the Indian rulers have the same posture: raised right hand (with a knife in it) with the left hand in a lower position (holding by the hairs the heads of the victims). This posture is copied by famous personalities: Napoleon, Washington, Adolf Hitler, Mussolini, the popes, etc. It is very famous, the Hitler salutation with the raised right hand, frequently with the right hand on the right side of the head and closed fist, holding something exactly as the Pharaohs were depicted in temples, the same posture used by the popes when blessing the multitude. The Statue of Liberty in New York has the same posture.

The wise men of the Vatican, including the popes of the eleventh, twelfth and thirteenth centuries, knew the identity of the beast 666, they knew that this beast was Solomon, and therefore they knew that the Temple of Solomon was not a holy temple. Those Vatican leaders planned and carried out the "Crusades," with the intention (among other things) of rescuing the Temple of Jerusalem from the Muslims (who at that time were in power in Palestine). The Temple of Solomon was destroyed centuries B.C. and later rebuilt by the Israelites who were freed in Babylon after the captivity. The Temple was destroyed again and was rebuilt by Herod the "Great" (father of Herod Antipas, who authorized the murder of Jesus Christ). Those popes made pacts with the Knights Templars (also called the Knights of the Temple of Solomon) in order to go together to Jerusalem to rescue the temple. The Knights Templars was a private religious and military order (soldier monks) approved by the papacy and obedient only to the pope (and not to any king or prince in any nation). It was the most rich and powerful private institution of those centuries. The spiritual father of the Templars was Solomon, so they loved the temple of Jerusalem (the Temple of Solomon).

At the beginning of the fourteenth century (in 1307), the Templars of France were arrested and many were executed; many escaped (especially to England). They were accused by the king of France, Phillip "the Beautiful," of worshiping the Devil. After being dismantled in France, they found refuge in several countries where they kept their money in secret places. They lived underground until they reappeared three centuries later with a new name: the Freemasons. This same king expelled the Jews from France and also went to Italy, arrested the pope, and put him in jail where he died a few months later. It was not a coincidence that this king fought against the Templars, the Jews, and the pope (I wonder if some person discovered the same secrets I am revealing in this book and told them to the king of France in 1307). This was not the only alliance of the popes with Satanists.

In consonance with their satanic beliefs, some leaders of the Vatican approved and promoted the horrible concept of the "transmutation of the blood and flesh of Jesus Christ." According to this Vatican idea, the ostia and wine taking during a mass physically and really become the blood and flesh of Jesus. I saw a picture in a Catholic newspaper showing the opened mouth of a parishioner who has blood and flesh of "Jesus Christ" after taking the ostia and the wine. This absurd idea is an imitation of the ancient pagan custom of eating the flesh of the sacrificed (ritual cannibalism). This concept is a subtle and subliminal manner of telling the Christian that even Jesus did a human sacrifice (with his own body).

The popes use a kind of cap (mitra) with two bands similar to the one used by Pharaohs with two bands also; the crook the popes use is like the one used by Pharaohs.

This is a picture (taken by the author) of the Dominican Pyramid (the Santo Domingo's Pyramid, or Columbus Lighthouse) in Santo Domingo, the Dominican Republic, where the author was born. This pyramid is the tomb of Christopher Columbus, who connected the Old with the New World.

20. The Apocalypse Revealed to Joaquin

The Apocalypse is a book of inspiration, which intends to give relief, strength and hope to the Christians. But the Apocalypse is also a book of HISTORY. This book speaks: 1) about Satan and warnings and threats given to him by angels, 2) the war of the angels against Satan and his followers, 3) the first and most famous pagan people, 4) the second defeat of Satan (in the future), and 5) the new Jerusalem (also in the future).

Throughout the book, John express terrible comdemnations against the rebel Jews and their spiritual leaders: David and Solomon. Three chapters are dedicated to revealing the satanism of Paul. The attack on the Judaists and Paul is the main issue in this book, probably a reflection of the bitter feeling that John carried as a consequence of the killing of Jesus by the Jews. (Today there is a revival of the old opinion of the Jews who say that Christ did not exist, that Christ was the creation of some Jew who had a problem with the Judaists of Jerusalem at the beginning of the first century. Today the Satanists and others called this opinion "the Quest for Jesus Christ.")

The Book of John (Apocalypse) is another clear proof against that theory; in any event, it is not a good thing to argue with Satanists. They know Jesus existed, but they made their choice: Satan.

Chapters 4 and 5 of Apocalypse speak about God and Christ. Chapters 6, 7, 8, and 9 speak in a figurative manner about the war of the angels against the Devil. Chapter 11 refers to Moses and Elias, two of the superheroes chosen by God to teach mankind the rules of peace and justice. These two prophets appeared to Jesus according to the Gospels, and John uses this theophany as an inspiration to write something about them. In this theophany were present Moses (representing the Law) and Elias (representing the Prophets). David and Solomon (representing the Books of Wisdom) were not present; clear indication that Christ rejected the Books of Wisdom and its representatives, David and Solomon. Throughout the book, John speaks about Egypt, Babylon, Rome, etc., making strong comdemnation of them.

The last two chapters, 21 and 22, are messages of hope to the Christians and the world.

In previous chapters of this book, I analyzed many verses of the Apocalypse and I explained their meanings. To understand the Apocalypse, we have to know the important key: JOHN WROTE THE APOCALYPSE TAKING IDEAS AND WORD(S) FROM THE OLD AND NEW TESTAMENTS, and the reason for this was that John wanted to reveal to the public (the Christian community) the satanism of David, Solomon, and Paul, and he could not do it clearly because the Jews would kill him easily (he was imprisoned on the Island of Patmos). In previous chapters I analyzed verses of the Apocalypse and showed the verses of the Old and New Testament related to them. I have a complete analysis of every verse of the Apocalypse, but I don't include them in this book because I don't have space.

21. Psychological Profiles of the Satanists

Egotism is one of the most important characteristics of those who follow the doctrine of "Wisdom." They are the only ones who should have wisdom and power according to the inner rules of their association. They, their families, and the members of their group are the only important persons in their lives; the others are important as far as they can be used to gain more power or to keep it. In order to do the last, they kill whomever, if necessary. They are hypocrites, cheaters, and liars. The predicament of "Equality, Freedom, and Fraternity," made public during the French Revolution, was a bait for the people, so they helped them to dethrone the king and get the power; as soon as they got the power, they installed the Reign of Terror in clear opposition to "Equality and Freedom." The "Fraternity" they proclaimed was really intended to be a fraternity for the members of satanic societies.

Egotism is in reality a feeling and an expression of an intrinsic and deep weakness of the personality. The egotists don't dare to endure or fight against the obstacles they face. They want everything for themselves to try to cope with personal, family, and professional situations and problems, and they try to control others so others don't fight against them. The egoists join other people with their similar weaknesses and desires in order to help each other. When they have to hurt others or kill others, they prefer to do it in groups, not only because they feel stronger when united, but also because when they kill, for example, the killing increases the cohesiveness and fidelity of every member of the group. If one of the members thinks to denounce a crime committed by another member, he does not dare to do it because he will be killed by the other members. For this reason the Masons are warned that they may be killed if they betray a brother(s). This is the way street gangs work in every nation.

Masons say that they work in order to reach national progress and personal perfection. These are lies intended to conceal their true goals. They lived attached to the ancient mysteries, which promoted human sacrifices, but they claim that they are the most advanced people on the planet. The minds of the Masons live in a pond filled with the blood of the millions they have sacrificed, but they said that they created the defense of human rights. They say that they are in possession of the "light," but they keep the world in ignorance through lies and dictatorships to avoid people knowing the truth about politics, history, and the activities of the Masons and other Satanists.

The Satanists have a limbic personality. They are still attached to the most primitive animal behavior, which includes violence and killing for survival or land control. The Christians have cortical personalities, they behave according to the teachings and the learnings that we analyze, accept, and keep in the cortical areas of the brain; and they use those learning as rules for living in peace and justice.

In modern times, the Satanists use all the instrument of power, like the mass media communications, to teach everybody that morality doesn't exist. They believe in "Situation Ethics," which teaches that nothing is wrong or bad (this idea is based in the "dualism" taught by Satan). And for this reason there is a generalized attitude in hundreds of millions of human beings, an attitude that is summarized by this expression used every day, everywhere: "I don't care"; most people don't care about the increasing perversions in all nations. They ignore that these perversions are an attempt to revive the Serpent's Empire.

Conclusion

I clearly showed in this book that almost all nations have been subdued to the will of Satan since five thousand years ago. Anyone can confirm my ideas by studying information that can be read in books, journals, newspapers, and other types of publications. If anyone studies this information and analyzes it according to the teaching of Jesus Christ, a conclusion can be easily reached: the unhappiness of millions of people is because the men in power, including the rulers, are not Christians, but anti-Christians. I have revealed secret information which help to expose the quasi-hidden satanism of the men in power who have ruled the world since the beginning of civilization. I exposed the continuous line of history of satanism, which started in Sumer and persists today. Now the readers have the necessary information in order to understand many historical facts and incidents that seem to be mysteries. The daily life of everybody on planet Earth is somehow affected by decisions taken by Satanists about the economy, politics, and religious activities.

If we want to avoid new wars and genocides, if we want to avoid the seizing of power by criminals like Hitler, Stalin, and Truman, if we don't want to see all the perversions of the current world, we have to: 1) know the truth that I exposed in this book, and 2) apply the teachings of Jesus Christ to live in a world of justice and peace. We have to face this reality: whether we live in peace according to the teachings of Jesus or live out the nuclear holocaust or total annihilation using modern arms of mass destruction. Now let the consciences of everybody tell them what to do concerning this great dilemma: Christianism or mass destruction. In my opinion, the decision and the work of the Christians and all the men with good hearts will prevail. And then, very soon, the Kingdom of Jesus Christ will be established in the whole planet and the habitable universe, forever.

Joaquin Caminero Guerrero
June 8, 1999
West Palm Beach, Florida, USA

Bibliography

A

Beginning, by Isaac Asimov. Berkeley Books, N.Y., 1989.
The Egyptians, by Cyril Aldred. General Editor: Glyn Daniel. Frederik A. Praeger, Publishers, N.Y., 1961.
Understanding the Old Testament, by Bernhard W. Anderson. Second Edition. Prentice Hall, Inc., New Jersey, 1966.
Asimov's Guide to the Bible, by Isaac Asimov, vol. 2. Doubleday and Co., Inc., N.Y., 1969.
The Secret Archives of the Vatican, by Maria Luisa Ambrosini with Mary Willis. Barnes and Noble Books, New York.

B

La Masoneria en Republica Dominicana, by Polanco Brito. Editora Amigo del Hogar, Santo Domingo, The Dominican Republic.
Ritual Instructivo del Mason, by Julio E. Baez. Talleres de la Editora Hermanos, Sto. Dgo., The Dominican Republic, 1975.
Por el Mundo de la Masoneria, by Pompilio A. Brower. Editora Montalvo, Sto. Dgo., The Dominican Republic, 1967.
The World of Indian Civilization, by Gustave Le Bon. Editions Minerva, S. A., Geneva, 1974.
El Vino a Dar Libertad a los Cautivos, by Rebecca Brown.
The Bible, Authorized Version; King James Version. Edited by Ernest Sutherland Bates, 1936, and also the edition of 1943.
The Story Bible, by Pearl S. Buck.
David, The Biography of a King, by Juan Bosch. Hawthorn Books, Inc., 1965.
The New American Bible (Catholic Biblical Association of America). P. J. Kenedy and Sons, 1970.
The Living Bible, paraphrased; Tyndale House Publications, Illinois, 1971.
The Reader's Digest Bible. General Editor: Bruce M. Metzger. The Reader's Digest Association, N. Y., 1982.

The NIV Study Bible, New International Version. General Editor: Kenneth Baker, Michigan, 1985.

In Old America (Random chapters on the Early Aborigines), by Walter Hart Blumenthal. Walton Book Co., N. Y., 1931.

Zoroastrians, Their Religious Beliefs and Practices, by Mary Boyce. Routledge and Kegan Paul, London, Boston, 1979.

The Dawn of Conscience, by James Henry Breasted. Charles Scribner's Sons, N. Y., 1933.

La Biblia. Ediciones Paulinas. Verbo Divino, Letra Grande, 1972.

Sagrada Biblia, by Nacar-Colunga, septima edicion, Biblioteca de Autores Cristianos, Espana, 1957.

Holy Bible, by Catholic Bible Publishers; Wichita, Kansas.

His Holiness, John Paul and the Hidden History of Our Time, by Carl Berstein and Marco Politi. Doubleday Publications.

A History of Egypt, by James Henry Breasted, second edition. Charles Scribner's Sons, N. Y., 1905.

Ancient Records of Egypt, by James Henry Breasted.

The Cultural Atlas of the World. Ancient Egypt, by John Baines and Jaromin Malek. Editor: Graham Speake. Publisher: Joseph J. Ward, 1984.

Egyptian Mummies, by Bob Brier, William Morrow and Company, Inc., N. Y., 1994.

Cuando las Piedras Hablan, by Rodolfo Benavides.

In the Shadow of the Temple. The Discovery of Ancient Jerusalem, by Meir Ben-Dov. Harper and Row, Publishers, N. Y., 1982.

Montezuma. Lord of the Aztecs, by C. A. Burland, G. P. Putnam's Sons, N. Y., 1973.

Rituales Masonicos, by Julio E. Baez.

C

The First Merchant Ventures, by Wiliam Culican. McGraw-Hill Books Co., N. Y., 1966.

The Realm of the Great Goddess, by Sibylle von Cles-Reden. Prentice-Hall, Inc., New Jersey, 1962.

Manual Masonico, by Andres Cassard.

The Encyclopedia of Monsters, by Daniel Cohen. Dodd, Mead and Co., N. Y., 1982.

A Comprehensive View of Freemasonry, by Henry Wilson Coil. Macoy Publishing and Masonic Supply Co., Inc., Virginia 1973.

Flags of the World, by Byron M. and G. Grosvenor.

Historia de las Religiones, by Carlos Cid.

Lost Lands and Forgotten People, by James Cornell. Sterling Publishing Co., Inc., 1978.

David, by Duff Cooper. Harper and Brothers Publishers, first edition, 1943.

America's First Civilization (Discovering the Olmec), by Michael D. Coe. American Heritage Publishing Co., Inc., 1968.

The Great Religions, by Richard Cavendish. Arco Publishing, Inc., N. Y., 1980.

Understanding the New Testament, by Howard Clark Kee and Franklin W. Young. Prentice Hall, Inc., New Jersey, 1957.

The Seven Wonders of the Ancient World, by Peter A. Clayton and Martin J. Price. Dorset Press, N. Y., 1988.

History of the Inca Empire, by Father Bernabe Cobo, translated and edited by Roland Hamilton. University of Texas Press, Austin, 1979.

Inca Religion and Customs, by Father Bernabe Cobo, translated and edited by Roland Hamilton. University of Texas Press, Austin, 1990.

Josephus. The Jewish War. General Editor: Gaalya Cornfeld. Zondervan Publishing House, 1982.

Napoleon on Napoleon. Edited by Somerset De Chair Cassel, 1992.

The Art of Ancient Peru, by Felipe Cossio del Pomar, 1971.

Lodestone and Evening Star. The Epic Voyages of Discovery, by Ian Cameron. E. P. Dutton and Company, Inc., N. Y., 1966.

Daily Life in Ancient Egypt, by Lionel Casson.

Nagasaki: The Forgotten Bomb, by Frank W. Chinnock. An NAL Book, The World Publishing Company, N. Y., 1969.

The Great Terror. A Reassessment, by Robert Conquest. Oxford University Press, 1990.

"The Initial Colonisation of the West Mediterranean Islands in the Light of Island Biogeography and Palaeogeography," by Dr. John F. Cherry. BAR International Series. *Archaeological Series* (National Maritime Museum, Great Britain), vol. 229, pages 7–27, 1984.

El Sagrado Coran. Edicomunicacion, S. A., Spain, 1986.

La Cohoba, by Jose A. Caro Alvarez, Sto. Dgo.

Los Tainos de la Espanola, by Roberto Cassa. Editora de la UASD, 1974.

"Human Genomic Diversity in Europe: A Summary of Recent Research and Prospects for the Future," by L. L. Cavalli-Sforza and A. Piazza. *European Journal of Human Genetics,* 1993; 1:3–18.

The Origin of Races, by Carleton S. Coon. Alfred A. Knopf, Inc., N. Y., Borzoi Books.

D

Dioses y Seres del Espacio en el Antiguo Oriente, by W. Raymond Drake. Edivision, Compania Editorial, S. A., Mexico, 1988.

Man Discovers His Past, by Glyn Daniel. Thomas Y. Crowell Co., N. Y., 1966.

The First Civilization, by Glyn Daniel. Thomas Y. Crowell Co., N. Y., 1968.

En Torno a Duarte, by Emilio Rodriguez Demorizi. Editora Taller, Sto. Dgo., R. D., 1976.

The Pyramids. An Enigma Solved, by J. Davidovitts.

The Heroes of Israel's Goldden Age. From Samuel to Micah, by George Dahl.

Conquistadors without Swords, by Leo Deuel. St. Martin's Press, Inc., N. Y.

German and Jew (The Life and Death of Sigmund Stein), by John K. Dickinson. Quadrangle Books, Chicago, 1967.

The Indestructible Jews, by Max J. Dimont. An NAL Book. The World Publishing Company, N. Y., 1971.

Biblical Numerology, by John J. Davis. Baker Book House, Michigan, 1968.

Keys that Unlock the Scriptures, by James E. Dean. E. P. Dutton and Company, Inc., N. Y., 1953.

Daily Life in Ancient Peru, by Hans Dietrich Disselhoff. McGraw-Hill Book Company.

The Aztecs, A History, by Nigel Davies. University of Oklahoma Press, 1920.

Tumultuous Years. The Presidency of Harry S. Truman, by Robert J. Donovan. W. W. Norton and Company, N. Y., London, 1982.

The Stars and Sripes, by Boleslaw and Marie-Louise D'Otrange Mastai. Alfred A. Knopf Publisher, N. Y., 1973.

Tutankhamen, by Christiane Desroches-Noblecourt.

The American Flag as Art and as History from the Birth of the Republic to the Present, by Boleslaw and Marie-Louise D'Otrange Mastai. Alfred A. Knopf Publisher, N. Y., 1973.

Discovering Ancient Egypt, by Rosalin David.

E

Ideas and Opinions. Albert Einstein, Editor: Carl Seelig. Crown Publishers, Inc., N. Y., 1982.

La Vida Gloriosa y Triste de Juan Pablo Duarte, by Rafael Estenzer. Editorial UNPHU, Sto. Dgo., R.D., 1981.

Tratado de Historia de las Religiones, by Mircea Eliade. Ediciones Era, 1964.

Mefistofeles y el Androgino, by Mircea Eliade. Coleccion Universitaria de Bolsillo, Punto Omega. Edicioines Guadanama, Madrid, 1969.

Lo Sogrado y lo Profano, by Mircea Eliade. Ediciones Guadanama, Lope de Rueda #13, Madrid, Espana, segunda edicion, 1973.

A History of India, by Michael Edmordes. Farrar, Straus and Cudahy, New York, N. Y., 1961.

A Century of Jewish Life, by Ismar Elbogen. The Jewish Publications Society of America, Philadelphia, 1944.

My People (the Story of the Jews), by Abba Eban. Behrman House, Inc., 1968.

How to Interpret the Bible, by James M. Efird. John Knox Press, Atlanta, 1984.

F

Python, by Joseph Fontenrose. University of California Press, 1959.

The Talmud for Today, by Rabbi Alexander Feinsilver. St. Martin's Press, N. Y., 1980.

The French Revolution, by F. Furet and D. Richet. The MacMillan Company, N. Y., 1970.

La Rama Dorada, by J. G. Frazer. Fondo de Cultura Economica, Mexico, 1944.

Extraterrestres y Creencias Religiosas, by Salvador Freixedo, Spain, 1971.

The Aztecs, by Brian M. Fagan. W. H. Freeman and Company, 1984.

George Washington and the New Nation, by J. T. Flexner. Little, Brown and Company, Ltd., 1970.

Saga America, by Barry Fell. Times Books, 1980.

America B. C., Ancient Settlers in the New World, by Barry Fell. A Demeter Press Book, 1976.

The Golden Bough. The Roots of Religions and Folklore, by James G. Frazer. Avenel Books, N. Y., 1981.

The Great Journey (The Peopling of Ancient America), by Brian M. Fagan. Thames and Hudson, Ltd., London, 1987.

Elusive Treasure (The Story of Early Archaeologists in the Americas), by Brian M. Fagan. Charles Scribner's Sons, N. Y., 1977.

Truman, by Robert H. Ferrell. A Centenary Remembrance. Thames and Hudson, Ltd., London; The Viking Press, N. Y., 1984.

The World of the Inca, by Bertrand Flornoy. The Vanguard Press, N. Y., 1956.

Off the Record. The Private Papers of Harry S. Truman. Edited by Robert H. Ferrell. Harper and Row, Publishers, N. Y., 1980.

The Rape of the Nile, by Brian M. Fagan. Charles Scribner's Sons, N. Y., 1975.

Maya Ruins in Central America in Color, by William M. Ferguson and John Q. Royce. University of New Mexico Press, 1984.

A People's Tragedy. A History of the Russian Revolution, by Orlando Figes. Penguin Groups, N. Y., 1996.

G

Your State Flag by J. R. Gebhart. Franklin Publishing Company, Philadelphia, 1973.

El Mexico Antiguo, by Paul Gendrop. Editorial Trillas, Mexico, 1974.

Quince Ciudades Mayas, by Paul Gendrop. Coleccion de Arte 31, UNAM, Direccion General de Publicaciones, Mexico, 1977.

Historia de la Salvacion, by F. J. Garralda. Editora Amigo del Hogar, Sto. Dgo., R. D., 1991.

History and Monuments of Ur, by C. J. Gadd. E. P. Dutton and Company, N. Y.

History of the Jews, by Professor H. Graetz, vol. 2. The Jewish Publication Society of America, 1895.

The Knight in History, by Frances Gies. Harper and Row, Publishers, N. Y., 1984.

Guerrilla Prince. The Untold Story of Fidel Castro, by Georgie Anne Geyer. Little, Brown and Company, first edition, 1991.

Near Eastern Mythology. Mesopotamia, Syria, Palestine, by John Gray. The Hamlyn Publishing Group Limited, 1973.

Islam. World Religion, by Mathews S. Gordon.

"Genetic Variations among the Mapuche Indians from the Patagonian Region of Argentina: Mitochondrial DNA Sequence Variations and Allele Frequencies of Several Nuclear Genes," by C. Ginther and others. *DNA Fingerprints: State of the Science,* ed. by S. D. J. Pena and others, 1993.

The Civilization of the Goddess, by Marija Gimbutas. Edited by Jaan Marlen; Harper Collins Publishers, 1991.

H

The Phoenicians, by Gerard Herm. William Morrow and Company, Inc., N. Y., 1975.

Wonders of the Past, by J. A. Hammerton, vol. 2. Wise and Co., N. Y., 1952.

Peoples, Seas and Ships, by Zvi Herman. G. P. Putnam's Sons, N. Y., 1967.

El Imperio de los Incas, by Victor Wolfgang von Hagen. Editorial Diana, Mexico, 1961.

Los Mayas, by Victor Wolfgang von Hagen. Mexico, 1968.

Los Reinos Deserticos del Peru, by Victor Wolfgang von Hagen. Editorial Diana, Mexico, 1973.

Man and the Sun, by Jacquetta Hawkes.

The Knight Templars, by Stephen Howarth. Atheneum, N. Y., 1982.

Natura y Cultura de las Islas Canarias, by Pedro Hernandez Hernandez, 1977.

Early Man in the Ocean, by Thor Heyerdahl. First edition in USA; Doubleday and Company, Inc., N. Y., 1979.

The Ra Expeditions, by Thor Heyerdahl. Doubleday and Company, Inc., Garden City, New York, N. Y., 1971.

The Ancient Sun Kingdoms of the Americas, by Victor Wolfgang von Hagen. The World Publishing Company.

The Last of the Incas, by Edward Hyans and George Ordish. Simon and Schuster, Inc., N. Y., 1963.

The Conquest of the Incas, by John Hemming. Harcourt Brace Jovanovich, Inc., N. Y., 1970.

Fingerprints of the Gods, by Graham Hancock. Crown Publishers, Inc., N. Y., 1995.

The Evidence of Earth's Lost Civilizations, by Graham Hancock. Crown Publishers, Inc., 1995.

History of Mankind. Prehistory and the Beginnings of Civilization, by Jacquetta Hawkes and Sir Leonard Woolley. Sponsored by UNESCO. Harper and Row, Publishers, N. Y., 1963.

The Emergence of Man. The First Cities, by Dora Jane Hamblin and the Editors of Time-Life Books, N. Y., 1973.

The World of the Bible, by Roberta L. Harris. Thames and Hudson, 1995.

I

Fair Gods and Stone Faces, by Constance Irwin. St. Martin's Press, N. Y., 1963.

Dragons and Dragon Lore, by Ernest Ingersoll. Payson and Clarke, N. Y., 1928.

Monuments of Civilization. Maya. Text by Pierre Ivanoff.

J

Mount Vernon. The Story of a Shrine, by Gerald W. Johnson and Charles Cecil Wall.

The Boat Beneath the Pyramid, by Nancy Jenkins. Holt, Rinehart and Winston; Thames and Hudson, Ltd., N. Y., 1980.

El Mito de los Padres de la Patria, by Juan Isidro Jimenes Grullon. Editora Cultural Dominicana, S. A., Sto. Dgo., R. D., 1971.

K

The Book of Signs, by Rudolf Koch. Dover Publications, Inc., N. Y., 1955.

The Brotherhod, by Stephen Knight. Dorset Press, 1986.

Lords of Sipan. A Tale of Pre-Inca Tombs, Archaeology, and Crime, by Sidney D. Kirkpatrick. William Morrow and Company, Inc., N. Y.

George Washington. The Pictorial Biography, by Clark Kinnaird. Hastings House Publishers, N. Y., 1967.

"Duarte, los Protestantes y la Masoneria," by Luis E. King. *"El Nacional"* newspaper, page 27, January 26, 1992, Sto. Dgo., The Dominican Republic.

L

Satan Wants You, by Arthur Lyons.

Brevario de Luz y Amor, by H. H. Lopez Penha. Editorial La Informacion, Santiago, The Dominican Republic.

Conversacioines con Juan el Vidente, by Javier Lopez. Editora Amigos del Hogar, Sto. Dgo., R. D., 1991.

La Revolucion Francesa y el Imperio, by George Lefebre. Fondo de Cultura Economica, Mexico, Buenos Aires, 1960.

Strange Sects and Cults, by Egor Larsen. Hart Publishing Company, Inc., N. Y., 1972.

Historia del Sionismo, by Waler Laqueur. Instituto Cultural Mexicano-Israel, 1982.

Petain: Hero or Traitor. The Untold Story, by Herbert R. Lottman. William Morrow and Co., Inc., N. Y., 1985.

The Faith of a Hasidic, by Max A. Lipschitz. Jonathan David Publishers, N. Y., 1967.

The Living Past, by Ivar Lissner. G. P. Putnam's Sons, N. Y., 1957.

M

Colon Llego Despues, by Jacques de Mahieu. Ediciones Martinez Rosa, S. A., 1988.

The Pleasure of Archaeology, by Karl E. Meyer. Atheneum, N. Y., 1970.

Historia de los Indios de la Nueva Espana, by Fray Toribio Motolinia. Author: Edmundo O'Sornan. Segunda Edicion, Editorial Porwa, S. A., Mexico, 1973.

Sociedades Secretas, by Norman Mackenzie. Alianza Editorial, Madrid, 1973.

Banderas y Escudos, by Ramiro Matos Gonzalez. Editora Libros, S. A., Sto. Dgo., R. D., 1981.

The New View Over Atlantis, by John Michell. Harper and Row, Publishers, San Francisco, 1983.

Age of the French Revolution. The Wind from America 1778–1781, by Claude Manceron. Vol. 1 and 2.

The Mystery of the Great Zimbabwe, by Wilfrid Mallows.

In Quest of the Great White Gods, by Robert F. Marx with Jenifer G. Marx. Crown Publishers, Inc., N. Y., 1992.

"Evidencia que exige un veredicto," by Josh McDowell. *Editorial Vida,* Miami, Florida, 1972.

House of Eternity. The Tomb of Nefertiti, by John K. McDonald. The Getty Conservation Institute and The J. Paul Getty Museum, 1996.

Red Land, Black Land. Daily Life in Ancient Egypt, by Barbara Mertz. Peter Bedrick Books, N. Y., 1978.

Discovering the Soviet Union, by Nikolai Mikhailov. Progress Publishers, Moscow, 1965.

Many Golden Ages, by Frank MacShane. Charles E. Tuttle Company, Publishers.

The Incredible Incas and Their Timeless Land, by Loren McIntyre. National Geographic Society. Washington, 1975.

The Riddle of the Pyramids, by Kurt Mendelssohn. Praeger Publishers, N. Y., 1974.

Why Hitler? The Genesis of the Nazi Reich, by Samuel W. Mitcham, Jr., Praeger Publishers, Westport, CT, 1996.

"Evolution of Modern Humans: Evidence from Nuclear DNA Polymorphisms," by Joanna L. Mountain and others. *Phil. Trans. R. Soc.* Lond. B (1992) 337, 159–165.

Milestones to American Liberty: The Foundations of the Republic, by Milton Meltzer. Thomas Y. Crowell Company, 1961.

Myths of Pre-Columbian America, by Donald A. Mackenzie. The Gresham Publishing Co., Ltd., London.

Flags of the World, by Byron McCandles and Gilbert Grosvenor. National Geographic Society, Washington, D. C., 1917.

In Search of the Indo-Europeans. Language, Archaeology and Myth, by J. P. Mallory. Thames and Hudson, Ltd., London, 1989.

N

El Leon y el Cordero, by John P. Newport.

Ancient America. Great Ages of Man. A History of the World's Cultures, by Jonathan Norton Leonard and the Editors of Time-Life Books, 1967.

185

O

Historia Universal, by Guillermo Oncken. Montaner y Simon, Editores, Barcelona, Espana, 1934.

South American Mythology, by Harold Osborne. The Hamlyn Publishing Group Limited, 1983.

P

La Francmasoneria, by Jean Palou. Editorial Dedado, Buenos Aires, 1979.

A History of the Jewish People, by James Parker. Quadrangle Books, Chicago, 1962.

Ancient Oaxaca, by John Paddock. Stanford University Press, California, 1966.

Asi Era Duarte, by Angela Pena. Editora Lozano, Sto. Dgo., R. D.

La Lucha entre el Poder Civil y el Clero. Mexico, by Emilio Portes Gil, Mexico, 1934.

The History of Anti-Semitism. From Voltaire to Wagner, by Leon Poliakov. Vol. 3. The Vanguard Press, Inc., N. Y., 1975.

Heraldry and Armor of the Middle Ages, by Marvin H. Pakula. A. S. Barnes and Co., Inc.

The Illustrated Guide to the Bible, by J. R. Porter. Oxford University Press, N. Y., 1995.

Francis Bacon and Secret Society, by Henry Pott. Francis J. Schulte and Co., Chicago, 1975.

The Library of Christian Classics. Vol. 15. *Luther: Lectures on Romans.* Edited and translated by Wilhem Pauck, Philadelphia. The Westminster Press, 1961; and also: *Luther's Meditations on the Gospels.*

Racial and Ethnic Differences in Disease, by Anthony P. Polednak, Ph.D., Oxford University Press, 1989.

Historia Universal, by Jacques Pirenne. Grolier International, Inc., Editorial Exito, S. A., Espana, 1972.

Q

Fidel Castro, by Robert E. Quirk. W. W. Norton and Co., N. Y., London, 1993.

R

A History of the Ancient World, by Mikhail Rostovtzeff. Greenwood Press, Publishers, CT, 1971.

Born in Blood, by John J. Robinson. M. Evans and Co., N. Y., 1989.

Buddhism, A Way of Life and Thought, by Nancy Wilson Ross. Alfred A. Knopf, N. Y., 1980.

Orpheus. A History of Religions, by Salomon Reinach. Liveright Publication Corp., N. Y., 1942.

Ancient Hebrew Seals, by A. Reifenberg. Horovitz Publishing Co., London, 1948.

Last of His Kind. An Informal Portrait of Harry S. Truman, by Charles Robbins. William Morrow and Co., Inc., N. Y., 1979.

Atlas of the Bible, by John Rogerson. An Equinox Book, 1989.

Codex Mendoza. Aztec Manuscript. Commentaries by Kurt Ross. Productions Liber S. A., CH-Fribourg, 1978.

People of the Nile, by John Romer. Crown Publishers, Inc., N. Y., 1982.

The Book of the Dead. Commentaries by Evelyn Rossiter. Crown Publishers, Inc.

S

The Dictionary of Ancient Egypt, by Ian Shaw and Paul Nicholson in Association with the British Museum. Harry N. Abrams, Inc., Publishers, 1995.

The Dragons of Eden, by Carl Sagan. Ballantine Books, N. Y., 1978.

Genesis and the Big Bang, by Gerald Schroeder. Bantam Books, N. Y., 1990.

The New Archaeology and the Ancient Maya, by Jeremy A. Sabloff. Scientific American Library. A Division of HPHL, N. Y., 1990.

A History of the Jews, by Frederick M. Schweitzer. The Macmillan Company, N. Y., 1971.

The Lost Realms, by Zecharia Setchin. Avon Books, N. Y., 1990.

Ancient Astronauts, Cosmic Collisions, by William H. Stiebing, Jr. Prometheus Book, N. Y., 1984.

Citizens. A Chronicle of the French Revolution, by Simon Schama. Alfred A. Knopf, N. Y., 1989.

Vida de Napoleon, by Stendhal. Coleccion Austral No. 1152, tercera edicion, Espasa-Calpe, S. A., Madrid, 1952.

Transformation, by Whitley Strieber. Wilson and Neff, Inc., 1988.

Everyday Life in Babylon and Assyria, by H. W. F. Saggs. G. P. Putnam's Sons, N. Y., 1965.

Egypt under the Pharaohs, by Barbara Sewell.

Guardians of the Universe?, by Ronald Story. St. Martin's Press, Inc., N. Y., 1980.

Possibility Thinkers Bible. The New King James Version. Executive Director: Robert H. Schuller. Thomas Nelson Publishers, N. Y., 1984.

Hanukkah. The Feast of Lights, by Emily Solis-Cohen, Jr. The Jewish Publication Society of America, 1937.

The Long Search, by Nimian Smart. Little, Brown and Co., Boston, Toronto, 1977.

The Religions of Mankind, by Hans-Joachim-Schoeps. Doubleday and Co., Inc., N. Y., 1966.

Biblical Historicism, by Clare Schumaker Roth. A Hearthstone Book, N. Y., 1972.

The Piebald Standard. A Biography of the Knight Templars, by Edith Simon. Little, Brown and Co., 1959.

The Aztecs, by Michael E. Smith.

Great Cities of the Ancient World, by L. Sprague de Camps. Doubleday and Co., Inc., N. Y., 1972.

Friends and Enemies, by Adlai E. Stevenson. Harper and Brothers, Publishers, 1959.

When Egypt Ruled the East, by George Steindorf and Keith C. Sule. The University of Chicago Press, 1942.

The Greatness that was Babylon, by H. W. F. Saggs. Hawthorn Books, Inc., Publishers, N. Y.

Egypt. Yesterday and Today, by Georgiana G. Stevens.

World History Series. *Egypt of the Pharaohs,* by Brenda Smith, Lucent Books, San Diego, California, 1946.

Sharing Secrets with Stalin, by Bradley F. Smith. University Press of Kansas, 1996.

"Human Fossils from the Endemic Island Fauna of Sardinia," by C. F. Spoor and P. Y. Sondaar. *Journal of Human Evolution* (1986) 15, 399–408.

Freemasonry. Its Hidden Meaning, by George H. Steinmetz. Macoy Publishing and Masonic Supply Co., Virginia, 1976.

Early Man in the New World. Edited by Richard Shutler, Jr. Sage Publications, Beverly Hills, California, 1983.

La Cultura Maya, by Laura Sotelo. Gobierno del Estado de Tabasco, Villahermosa, Mexico, 1986.

La Universidad Autonoma de Santo Domingo y Duarte, Duarte Fundador de la Republica?, by Jose Anibal Sanchez Fernandez. Editora Alfa y Omega., Sto. Dgo., R.D., 1980.

T

The History of Buddhist Thought, by Edward J. Thomas. Alfred A. Knopf, N. Y., 1933.

Descripcion e Historia del Reino de las Islas Canarias, by Leonardo Torriani. Goya Ediciones, Santa Cruz de Tenerife, Islas Canarias, 1959.

The Rise and Fall of Maya Civilization, by Eric Thompson. Second Edition. University of Oklahoma Press, 1966.

Monarquia Indiana, by Fray Juan de Torquemada. Universidad Nacional Autonoma de Mexico, Mexico, 1964.

El Misterio de las Piramides, Mexicanas, by Peter Tompkins. Editorial Diana, Mexico, 1989.

Secrets of the Great Pyramids, by Peter Tompkins, Harper and Row, Publishers, 1971.

The Magic of Obelisks, by Peter Tompkins. Harper and Row, Publishers, N. Y., 1981.

Life World Library. *Russia,* by Charles W. Thayer and the Editors of Life. Time Inc., N. Y., 1965.

The American Discovery of Ancient Egypt, by Nancy Thomas. Harry N. Abrahams, Inc., N. Y., 1995.

"Native American Mitochondrial DNA Analysis indicates that the Amerinds and the Nadene Populations Were Founded by Two Independent Migrations," by Antonio Torroni and others. *Genetics* 130:153–162 (January, 1992).

Conquest, Montezuma, Cortes, and the Fall of Old Mexico, by Hugh Thomas. Simon and Schuster, Inc., 1993.

Maya, History and Religion, by J. Eric S. Thompson. University of Oklahoma Press, 1970.

V

Confrontations, by Jacques Valle, Random House, Inc., Ballantine Books, N. Y., 1990.

Heraldry, Customs, Rules and Styles, by Carl-Alexander von Valborth. Blandford Books, Ltd., 1981.

People of the Seas, by Immanuel Velikovsky. Doubleday and Co., Inc., Garden City, N. Y., 1977.

Duarte, Apostol y Libertador, by Pedro R. Vasquez, Editora Lazaro, C x A, Sto. Dgo., R. D., 1980.

W

History Was Buried, by Margaret Wheeler. Hart Publishing Company, Inc., N. Y., 1967.

The Gods of Ancient Egypt, by Barbara Watherson. Editor: Facts on Life, N. Y., 1984.

An Introduction to American Archaeology, vol. 1, by Gordon R. Willey, 1966.

The French Revolution. A Study in Democracy, by Nesta H. Webster.

Cleopatra's Needles and Other Egyptian Obelisks, by E. A. Wallis Budge. Dover Publications, Inc., N. Y., 1990.

Tutankhamen, by Sir Ernest A. Wallils Budge. Bell Publishing Co., N. Y., 1990.

The Book of the Dead, translated by E. A. Wallis Budge.

"American Indian Prehistory as Written in the Metochondrial DNA:" A Review, by Douglas C. Wallace and Antonio Torroni. *Human Biology,* June 1992, vol. 64, No. 3, pp. 403–416.

The Complete Works of Josephus. Flavius Josephus. Translated by Wm. Whiston. Kregel Publications, 1981.

Z

Heraldry in America, by Eugene Zieber. Greenwich House. Crown Publishers, Inc., 1984.

Others:

"El Faro a Colon." *Revista del Comite Ejecutivo Permanente del Faro a Colon,* #3, 5, 19, 21, 23 y 24, Sto. Dgo., R. D.

Revista de la Gran Logia de la Republica Dominicana, Sept., 1982.

The Holy Scriptures. According to the Masoretic Text. The Jewish Publication Society of America.

The Boat Beneath the Pyramid. King Cheops' Royal Ship. Holt, Rinehart and Winston, N. Y., 1980.

Reader's Digest. *Mysteries of the Ancient Americas. The New World Before Columbus.* The Reader's Digest Association, Inc., 1986.

Reader's Digest, *Mysteries of the Bible.* The Reader's Digest Association.

The World Almanac and Book of Facts, 1996.

Incas: Lords of Gold and Glory. Time-Life Books, 1992.

Aztecs: Reign of Blood and Splendor. Lost Civilizations. Time-Life Books, 1992.

The Horizon Book of Lost Worlds, by The Editors of Horizon Magazine. American Heritage Publishing, Co., Inc., N. Y., 1962.

Mexican and Central American Mythology. Newness Books, 1993.

What Life Was Like on the Banks of the Nile. Time-Life Books, 1996.

The "SS," by the Editors of Time-Life Books, Alexandria, Virginia.

Los Testigos de Jehova. Watch Tower Bible and Tract Society of Pennsylvania, 1993.

The Genetics of Migrant and Isolated Populations. The Williams and Wilkins Co., 1963.

Indians of the Americas. National Geographic Society, fourth edition, Washington, D.C., 1958.

Itinerario Documental de Simon Bolivar. Escritos Selectos. Republica de Venezuela; Ediciones de la Presidencia. Caracas, 1970.

Apuntes en Torno a la Mitologia de los Indios Tainos de las Antillas Mayores y sus Origenes Suramericanos. Centro de Estudios Avanzados de Puerto Rico y el Caribe. Museo del Hombre Dominicano, Sto. Dgo., R. D., 1978.